MILK
PEACH
BANAN

CAT & CAT ADVENTURES
The Goblet of Infinity

SUSIE YI

HARPER alley

An Imprint of HarperCollinsPublishers

Thank you to my family, Jack Gang, Yeon Yi, Man Jae Yi, and Heidi Yi, as well as my wonderful agent, Kathleen Ortiz, and the amazing team at HarperAlley who have made this book possible.

HarperAlley is an imprint of HarperCollins Publishers.
Cat & Cat Adventures: The Goblet of Infinity
Copyright © 2021 by Susie Yi.
All rights reserved. Manufactured in Italy.
www.harperalley.com
ISBN 978-0-06-308384-4 — ISBN 978-0-06-308383-7 (pbk.)

The artist used a computer, tablet, and the endless source of energy that only cats sitting in your lap can provide to create the digital illustrations for this book.

Typography by Susie Yi
22 23 24 25 26 RTLO 10 9 8 7 6 5 4 3 2 1
❖
First Edition

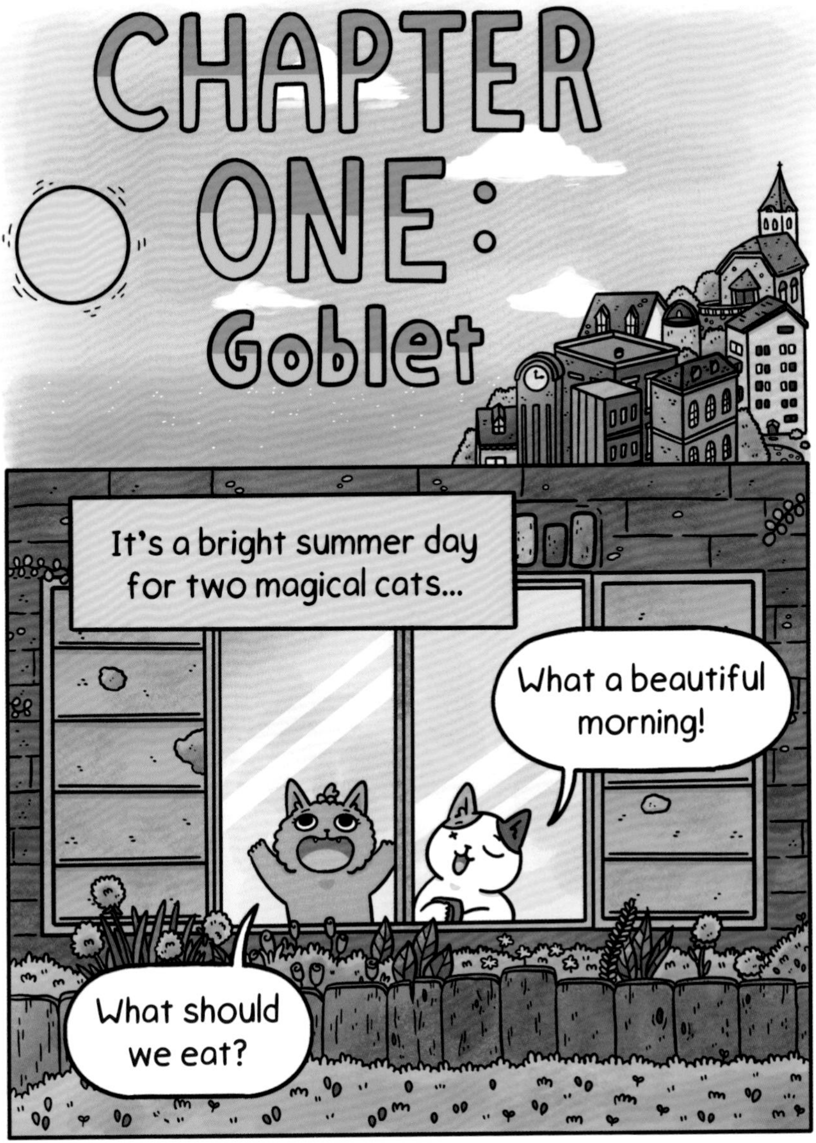
CHAPTER ONE:
Goblet
It's a bright summer day for two magical cats...
What a beautiful morning!
What should we eat?

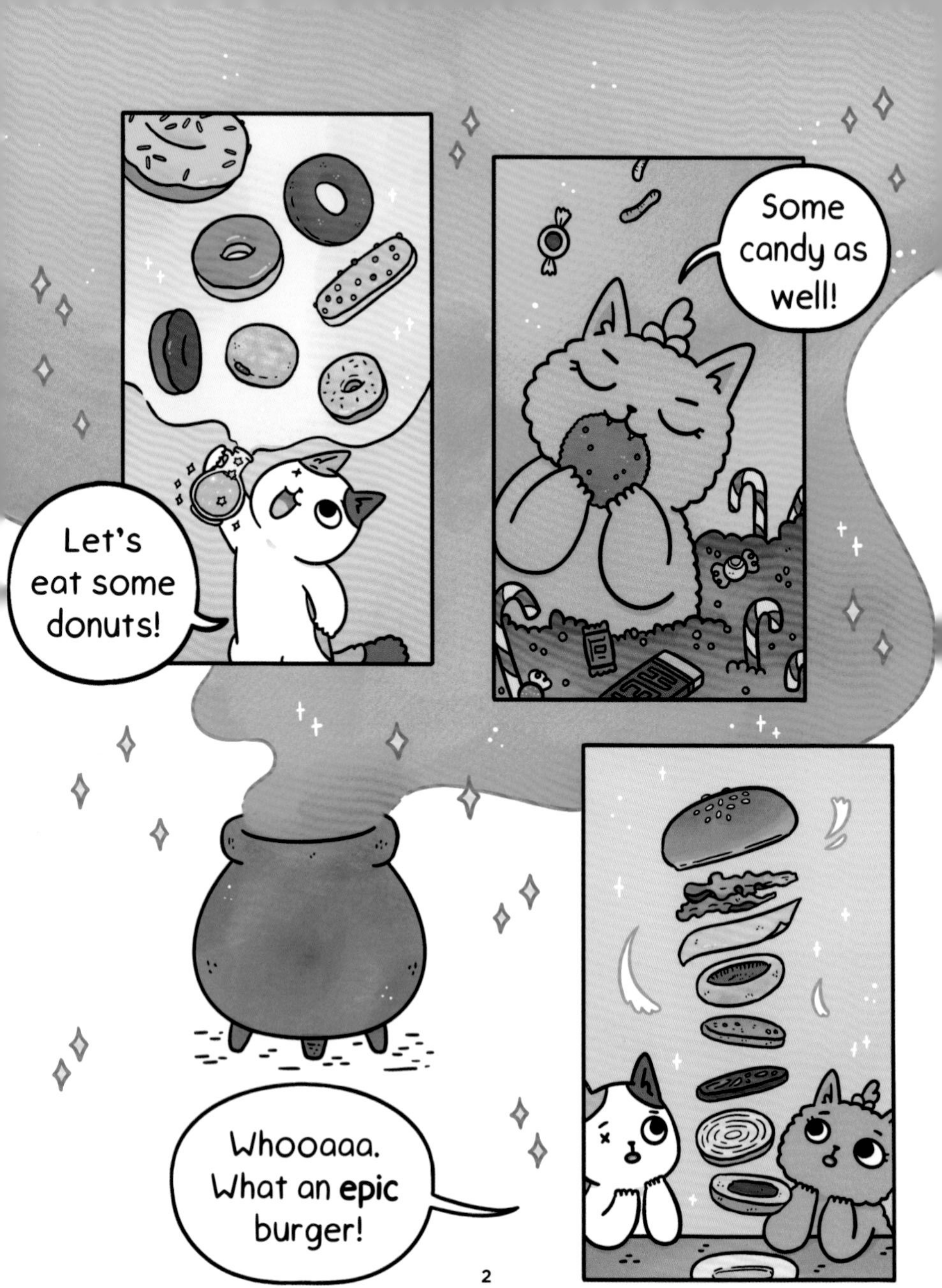
Let's eat some donuts!
Some candy as well!
Whooaaa. What an epic burger!

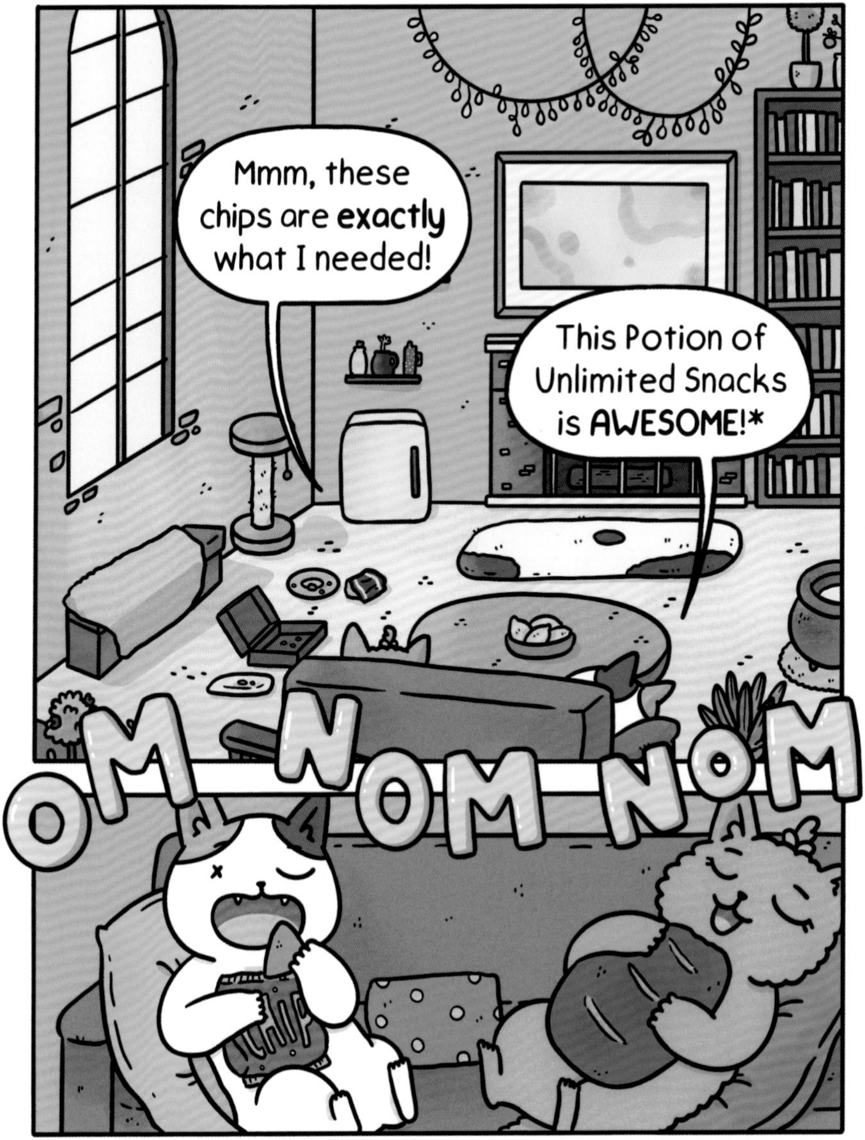
Mmm, these chips are **exactly** what I needed!
This Potion of Unlimited Snacks is **AWESOME!***
OM NOM OM NOM NOM

*See *Cat & Cat Adventures: The Quest for Snacks*

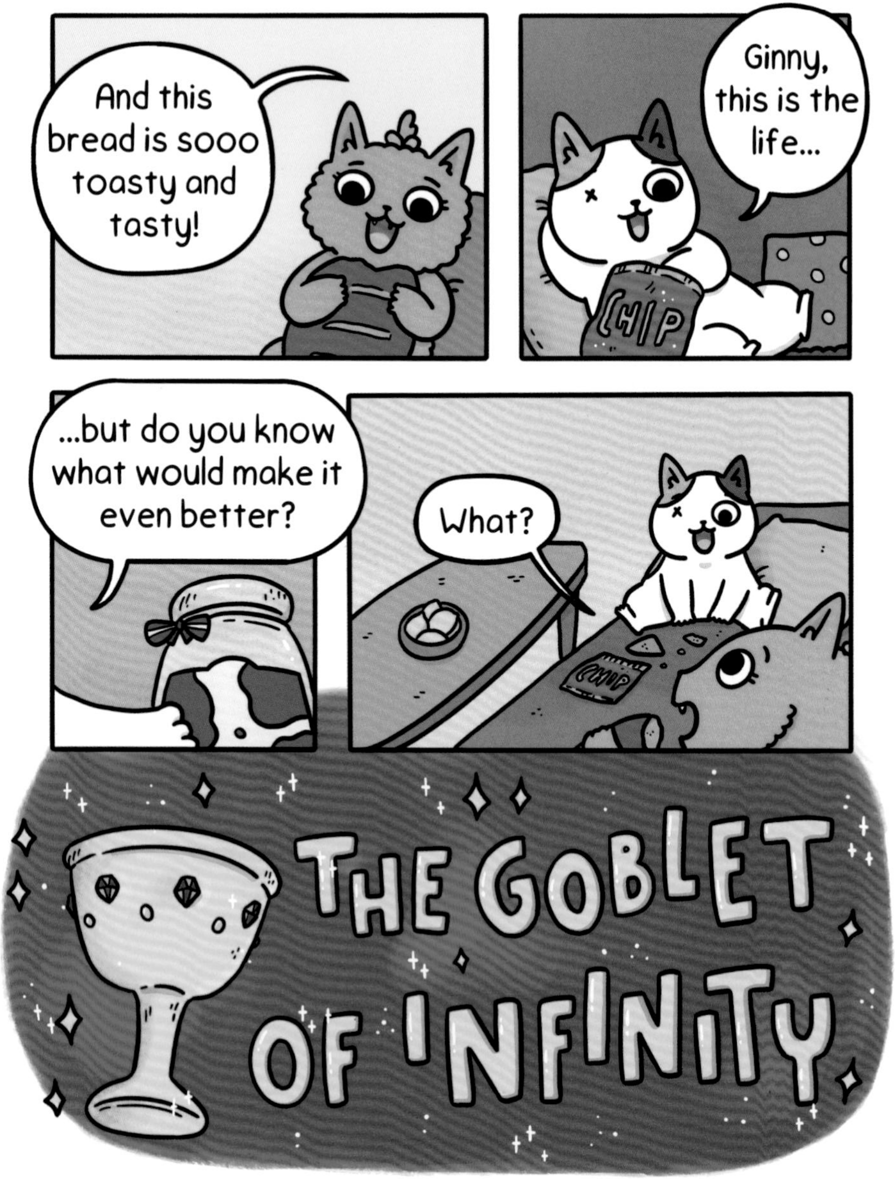
And this bread is sooo toasty and tasty!
Ginny, this is the life...
CHIP
...but do you know what would make it even better?
What?
CHIP
THE GOBLET OF INFINITY

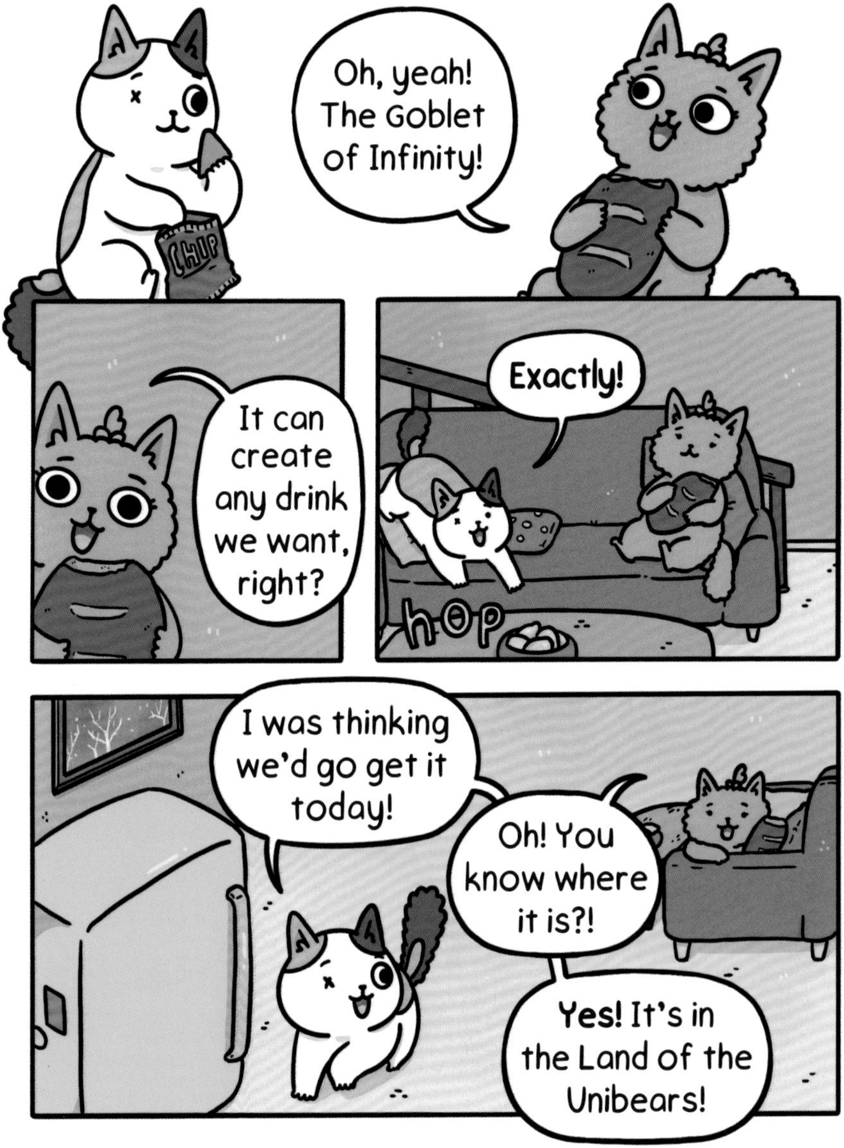
Oh, yeah! The Goblet of Infinity!
CHIP
It can create any drink we want, right?
Exactly!
hop
I was thinking we'd go get it today!
Oh! You know where it is?!
Yes! It's in the Land of the Unibears!

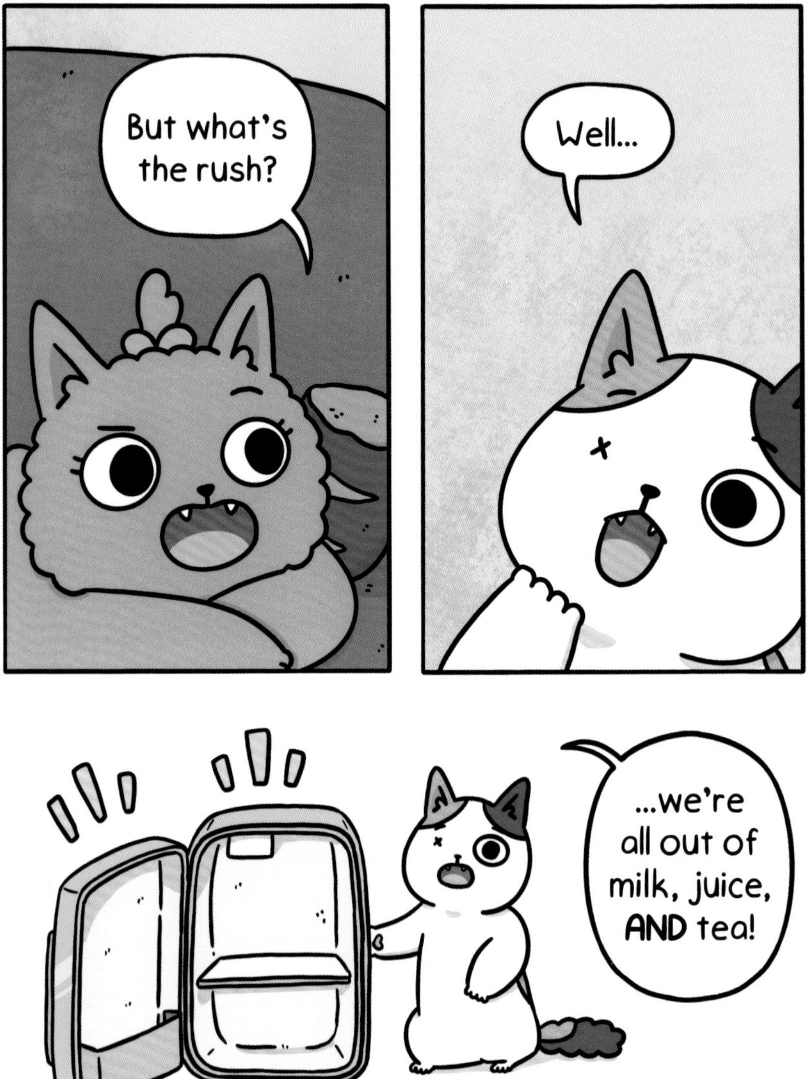
But what's the rush?
Well...
...we're all out of milk, juice, AND tea!

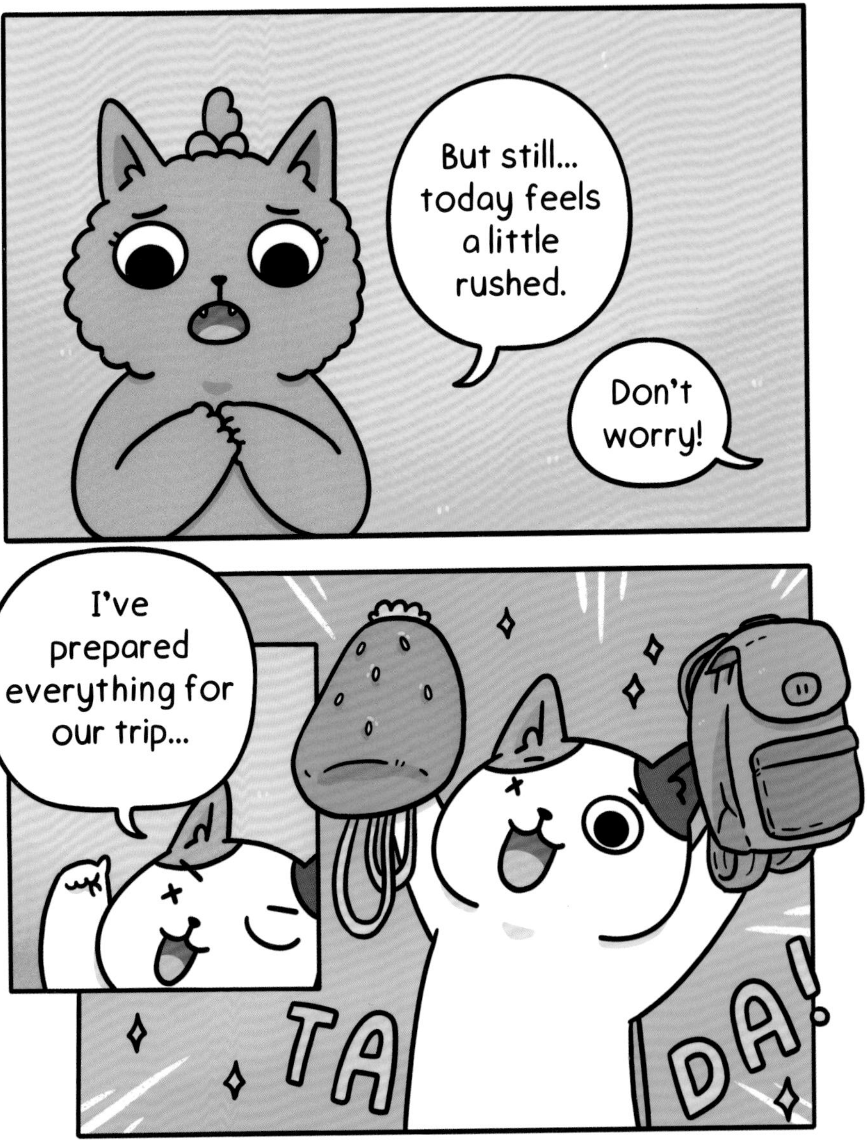

But still... today feels a little rushed.
Don't worry!
I've prepared everything for our trip...
TA DA!

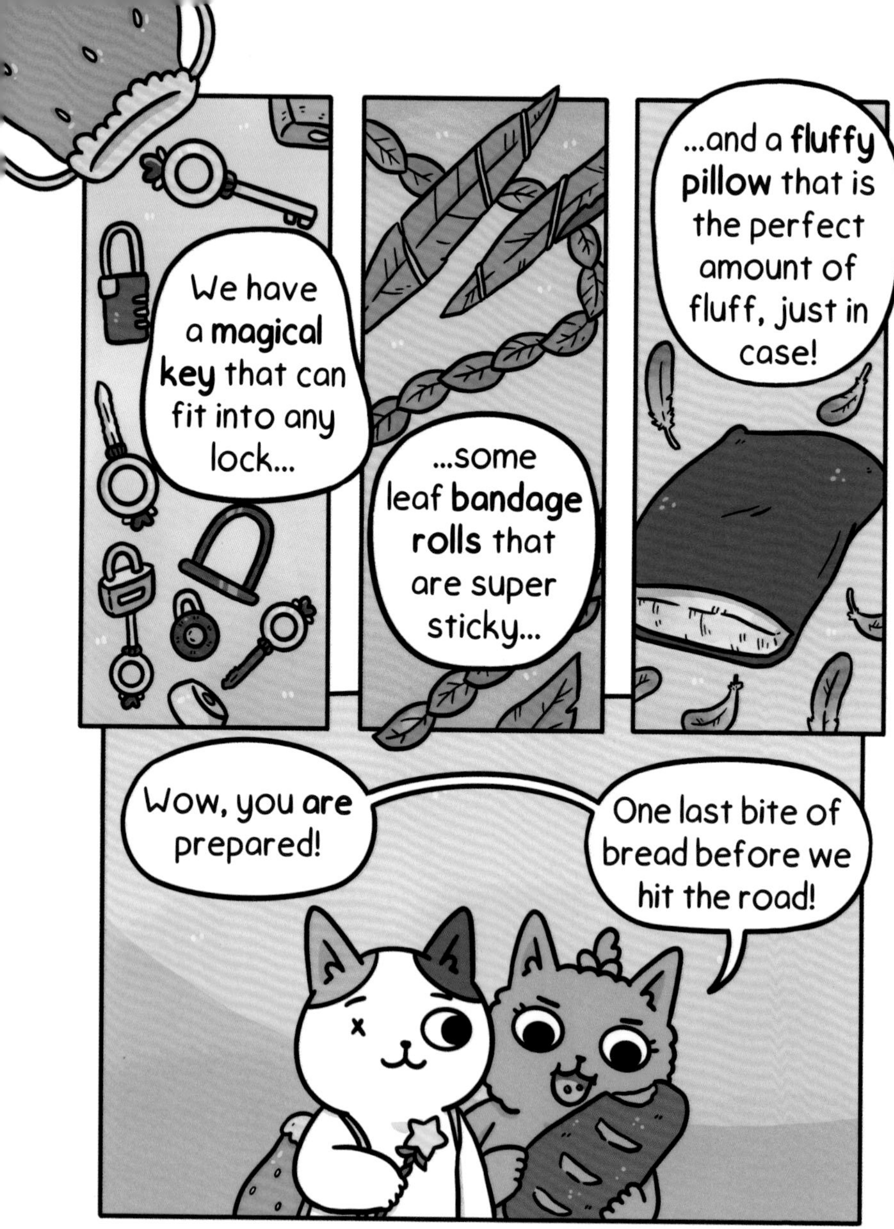
We have a **magical key** that can fit into any lock...
...some leaf **bandage rolls** that are super sticky...
...and a **fluffy pillow** that is the perfect amount of fluff, just in case!
Wow, you **are** prepared!
One last bite of bread before we hit the road!

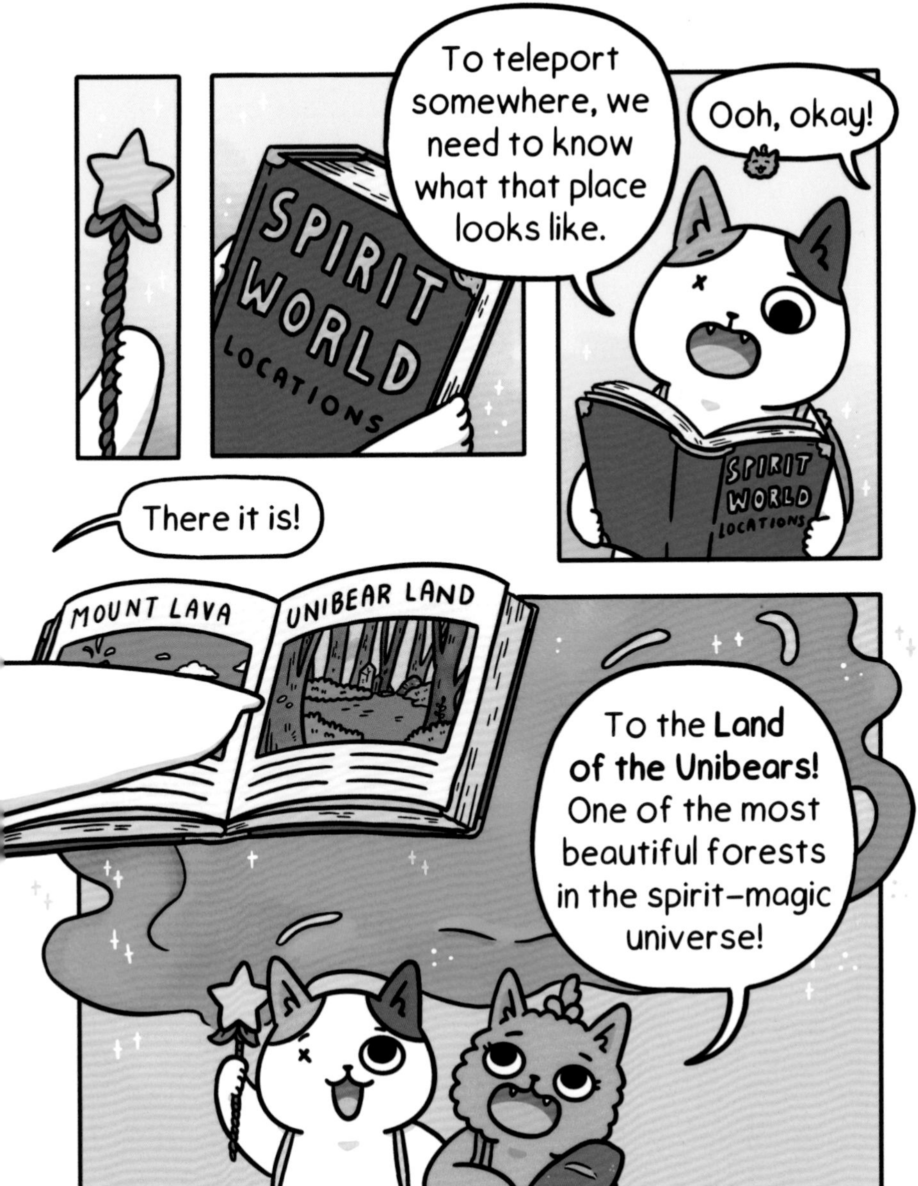

To teleport somewhere, we need to know what that place looks like.
SPIRIT WORLD LOCATIONS
Ooh, okay!
SPIRIT WORLD LOCATIONS
There it is!
MOUNT LAVA
UNIBEAR LAND
To the **Land of the Unibears!** One of the most beautiful forests in the spirit-magic universe!

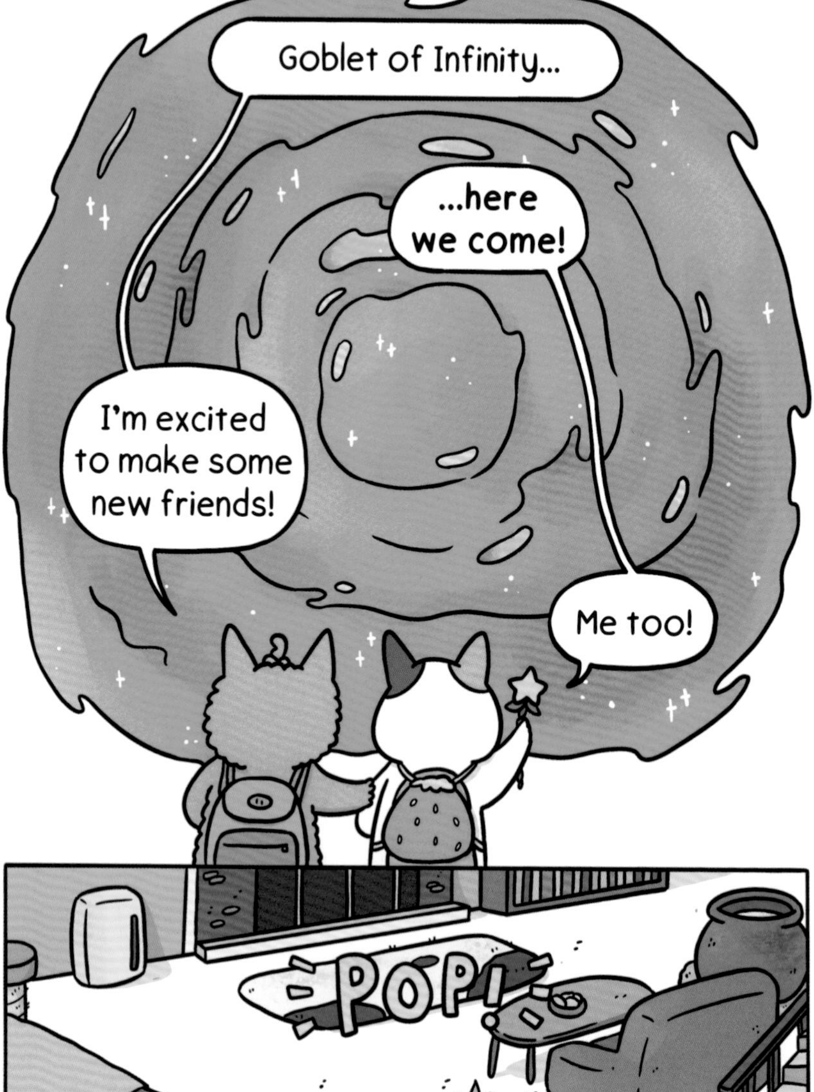
Goblet of Infinity...
...here we come!
I'm excited to make some new friends!
Me too!
POP!

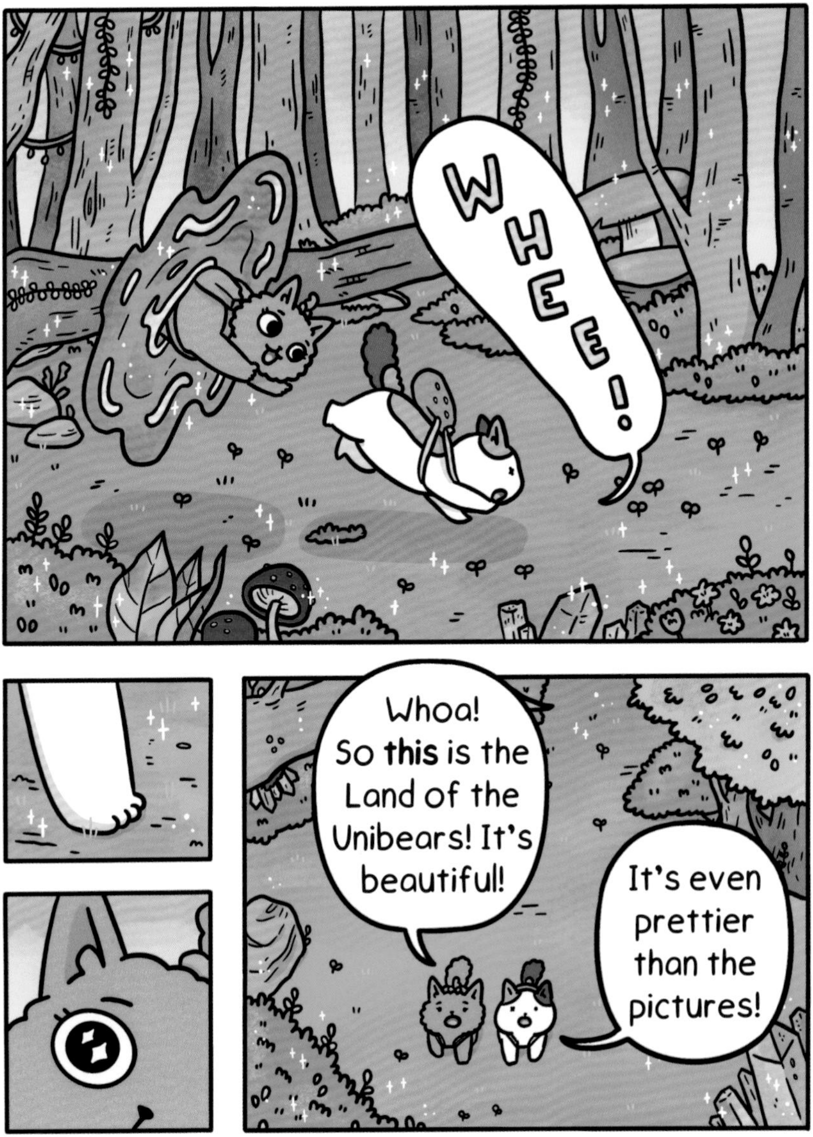
WHEE!
Whoa! So **this** is the Land of the Unibears! It's beautiful!
It's even prettier than the pictures!

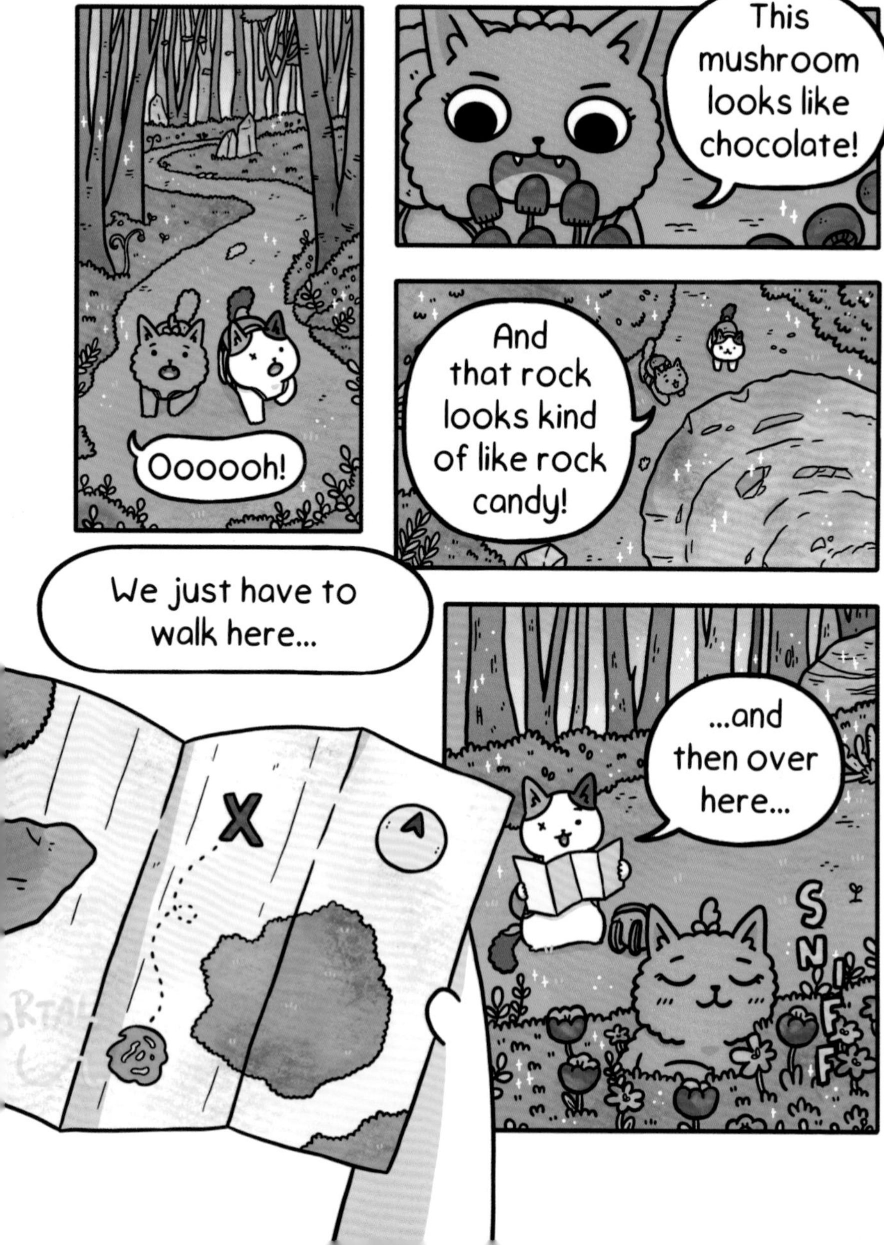
Oooooh!
This mushroom looks like chocolate!
And that rock looks kind of like rock candy!
We just have to walk here...
...and then over here...
SNIFF

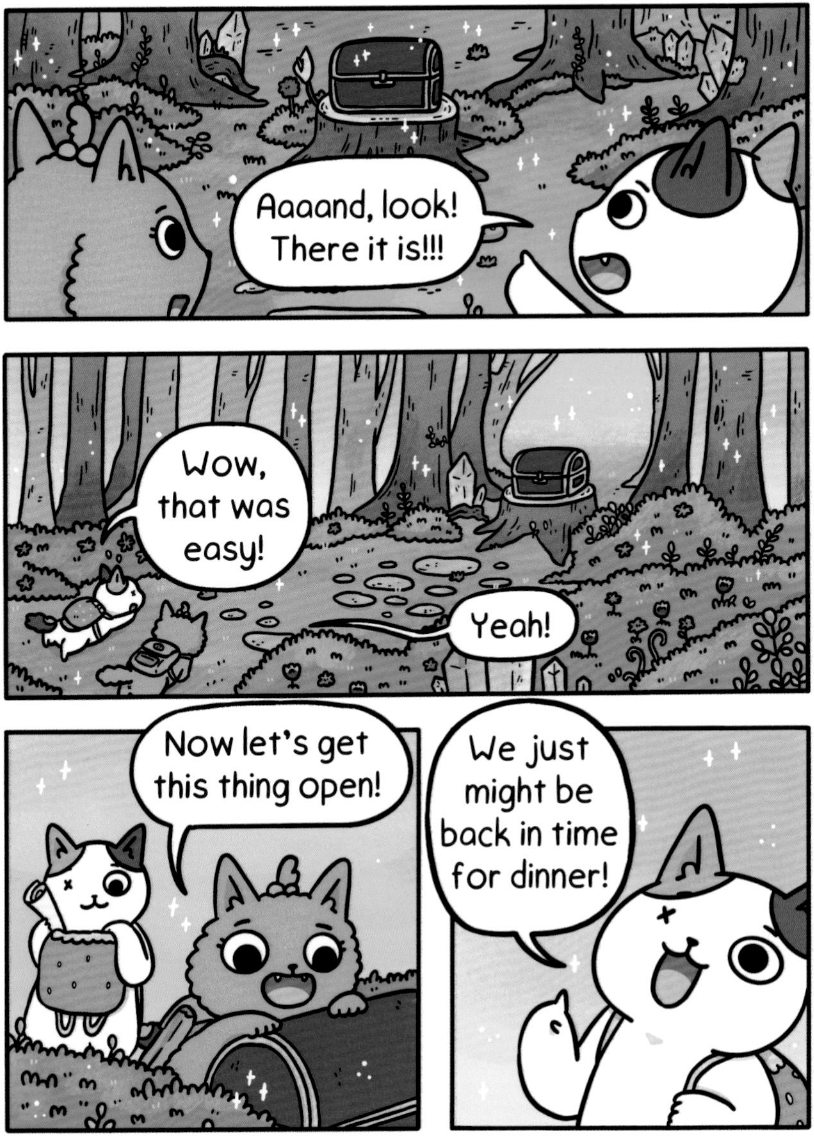
Aaaand, look! There it is!!!
Wow, that was easy!
Yeah!
Now let's get this thing open!
We just might be back in time for dinner!

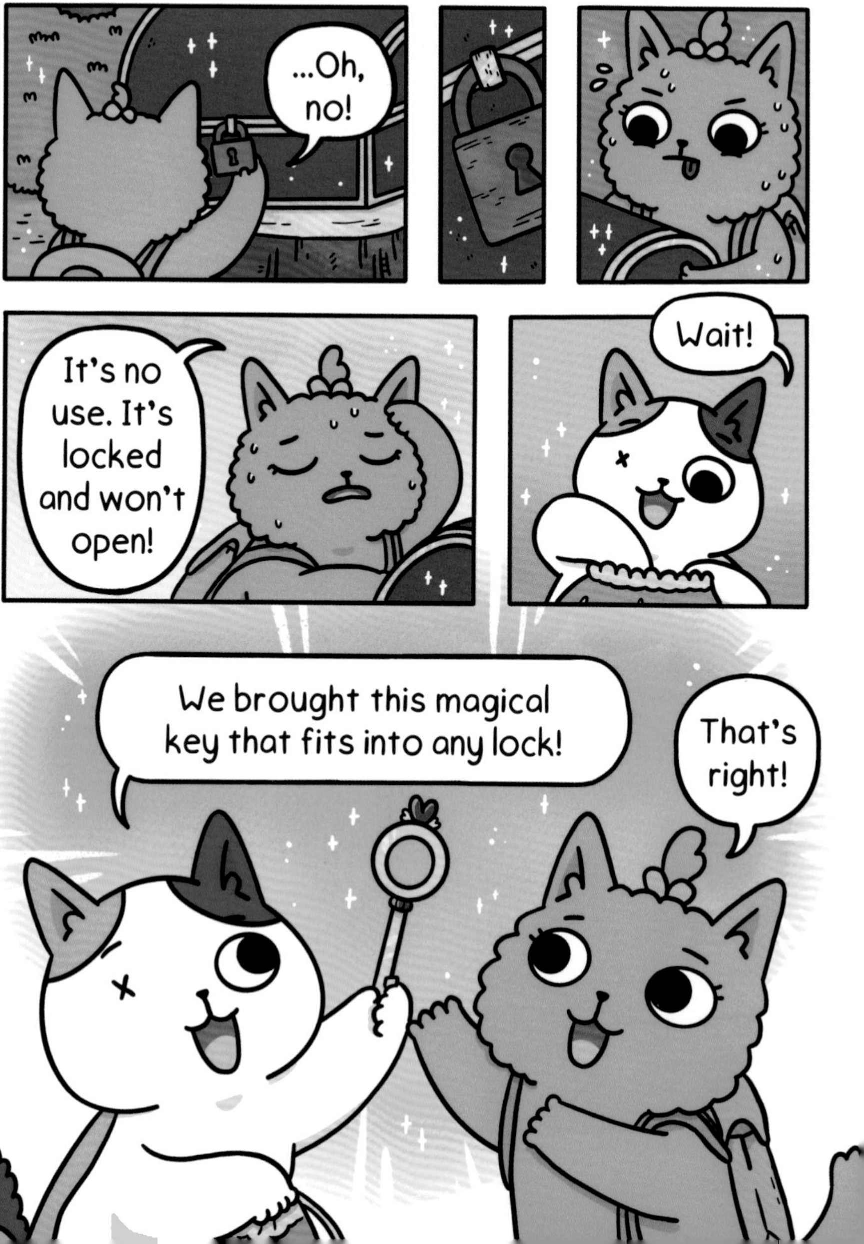
...Oh, no!
It's no use. It's locked and won't open!
Wait!
We brought this magical key that fits into any lock!
That's right!

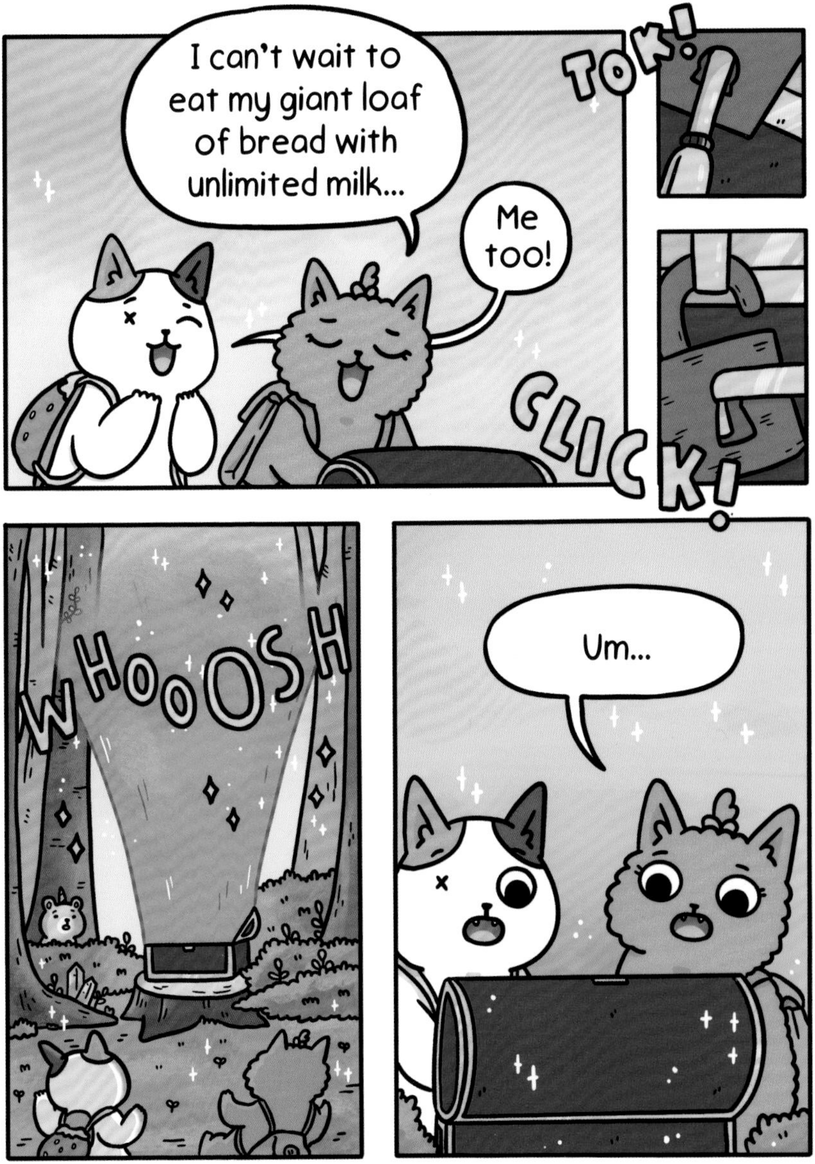
I can't wait to eat my giant loaf of bread with unlimited milk...
Me too!
TOK!
CLICK!
WHOOOSH
Um...

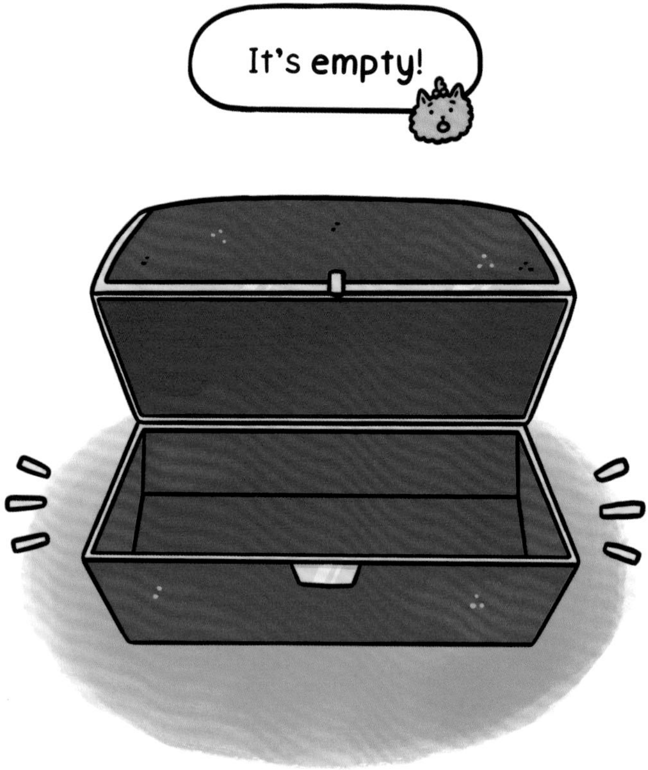
It's empty!

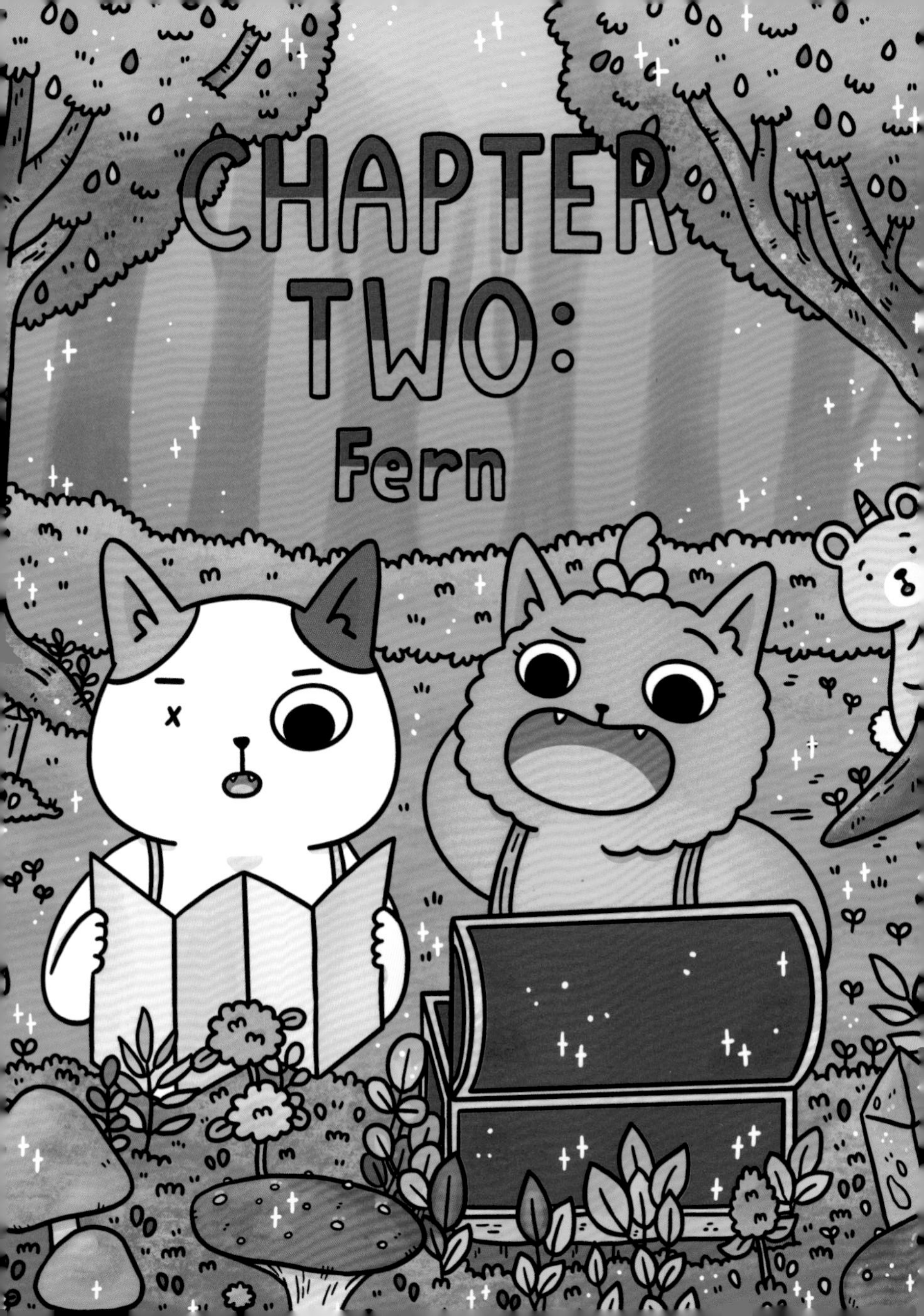
CHAPTER TWO:
Fern

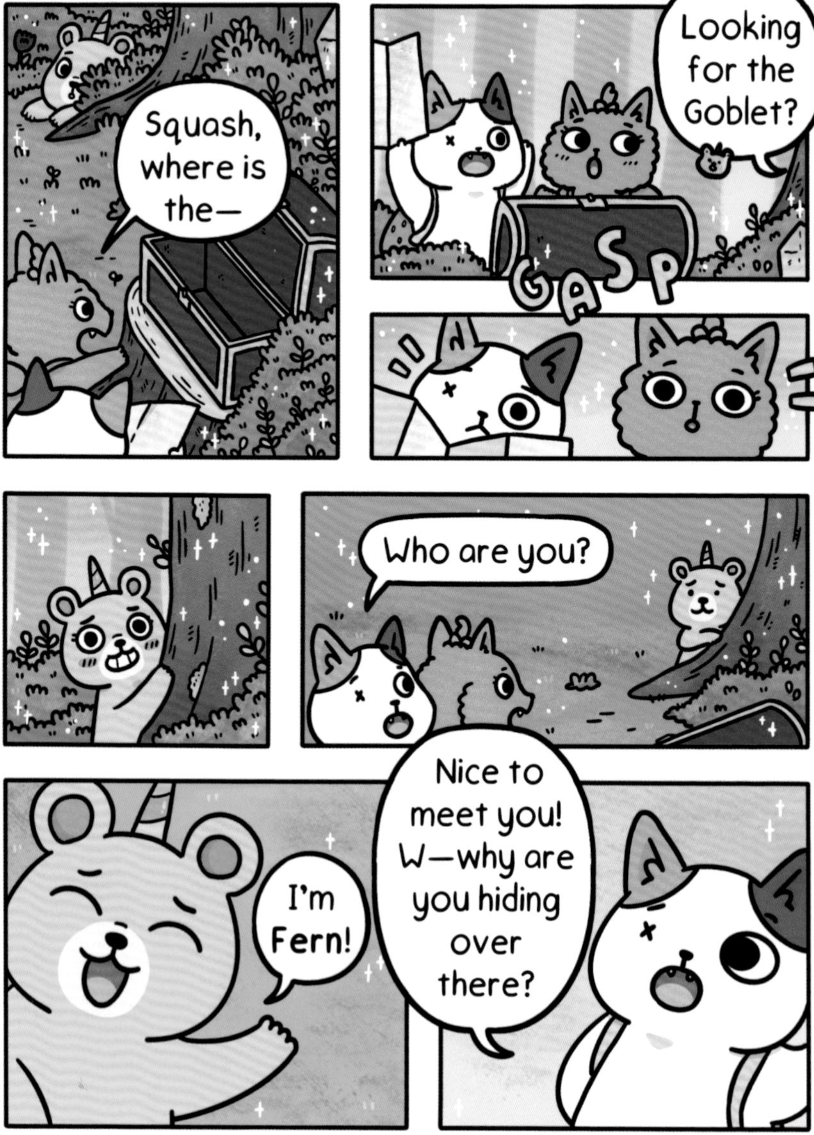
Squash, where is the—
Looking for the Goblet?
GASP
Who are you?
I'm Fern!
Nice to meet you! W—why are you hiding over there?

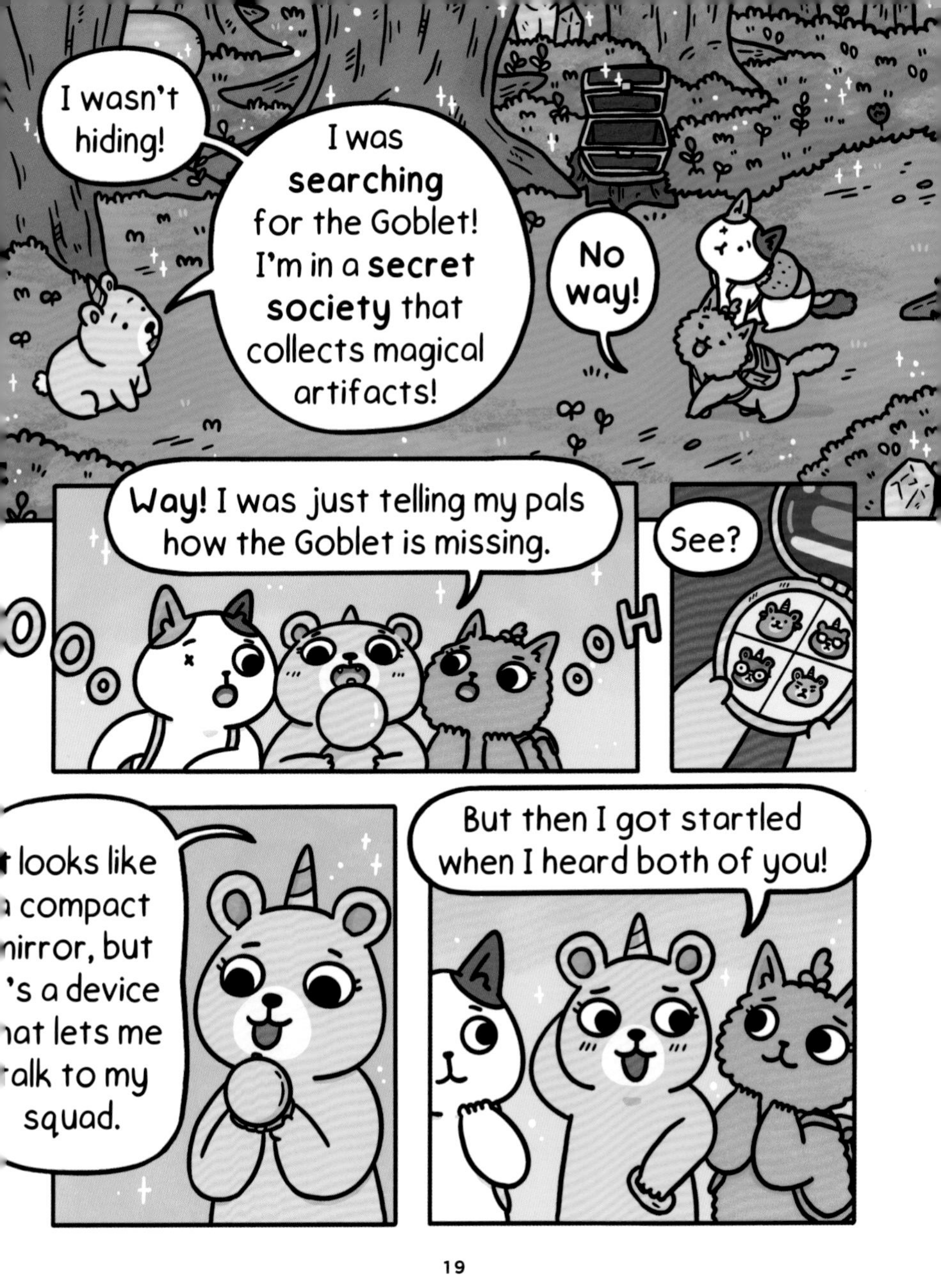
I wasn't hiding!
I was searching for the Goblet! I'm in a secret society that collects magical artifacts!
No way!
Way! I was just telling my pals how the Goblet is missing.
OOOOOOH
See?
looks like
compact
irror, but
's a device
at lets me
alk to my
squad.
But then I got startled when I heard both of you!

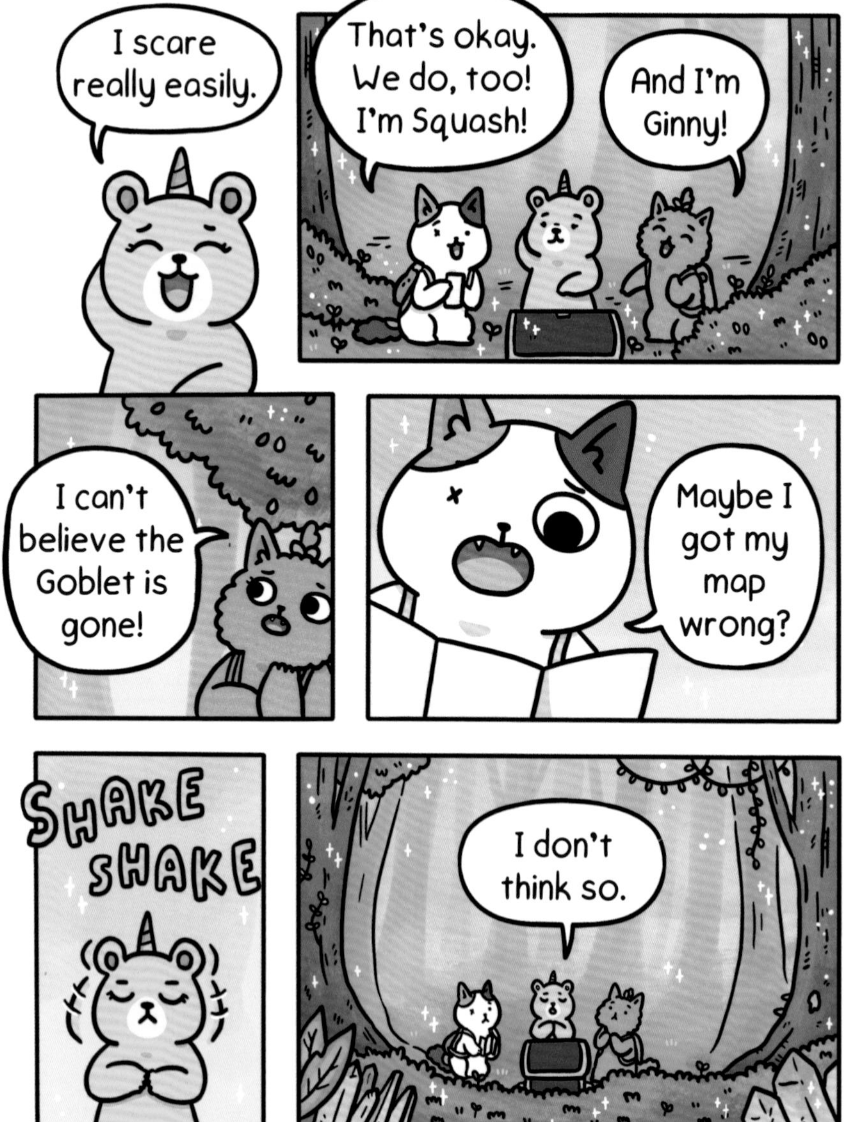
I scare really easily.
That's okay. We do, too! I'm Squash!
And I'm Ginny!
I can't believe the Goblet is gone!
Maybe I got my map wrong?
SHAKE SHAKE
I don't think so.

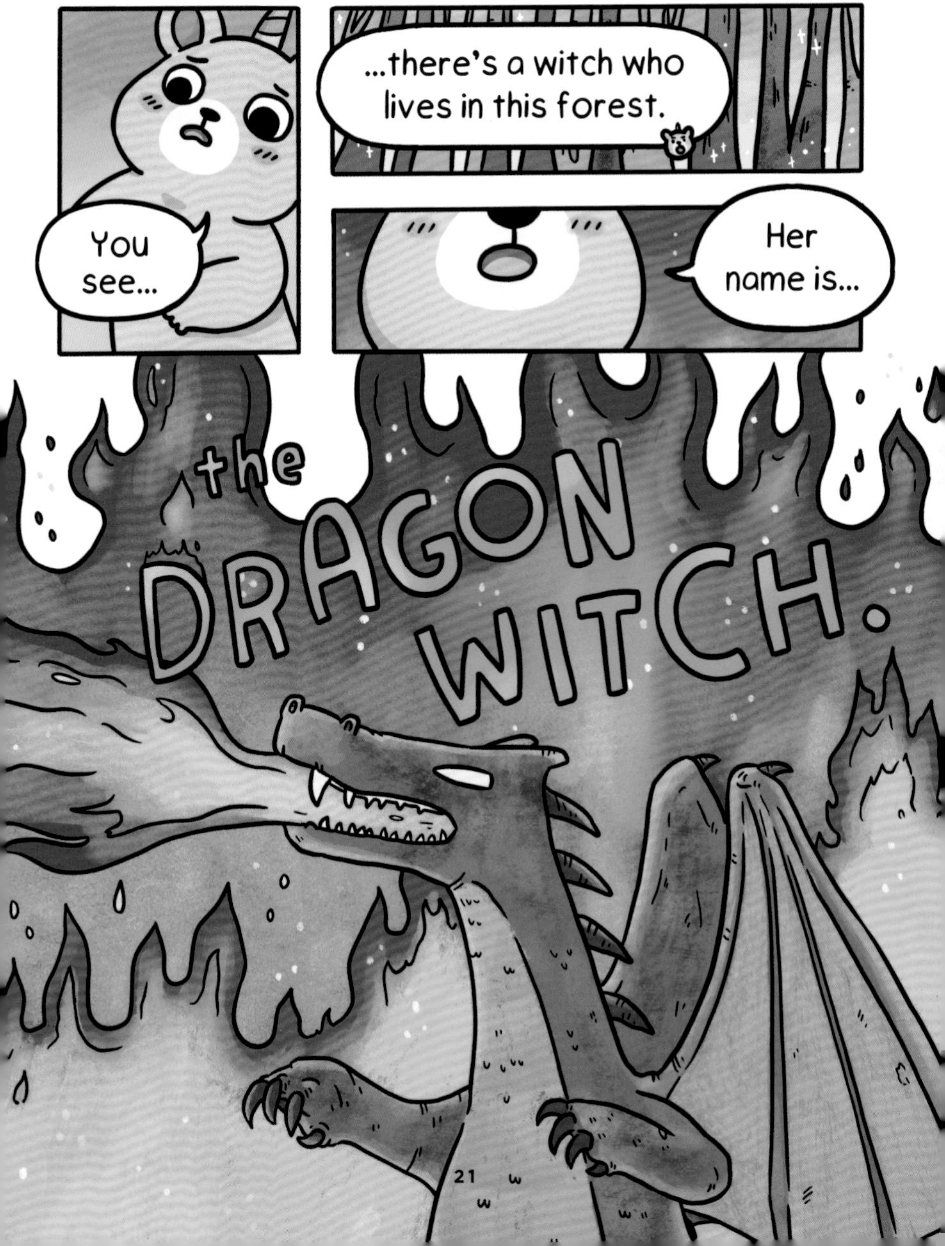
You see...
...there's a witch who lives in this forest.
Her name is...
the DRAGON WITCH.

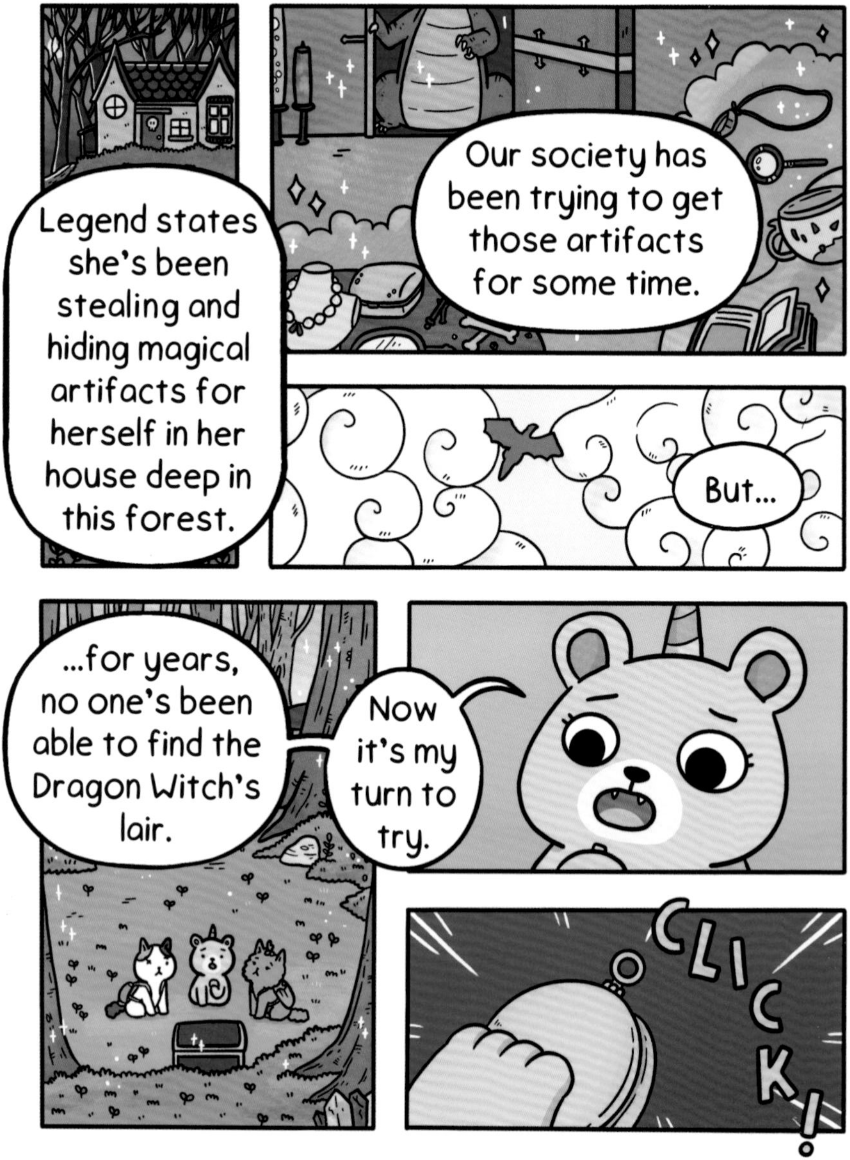
Legend states she's been stealing and hiding magical artifacts for herself in her house deep in this forest.
Our society has been trying to get those artifacts for some time.
But...
...for years, no one's been able to find the Dragon Witch's lair.
Now it's my turn to try.
CLICK!

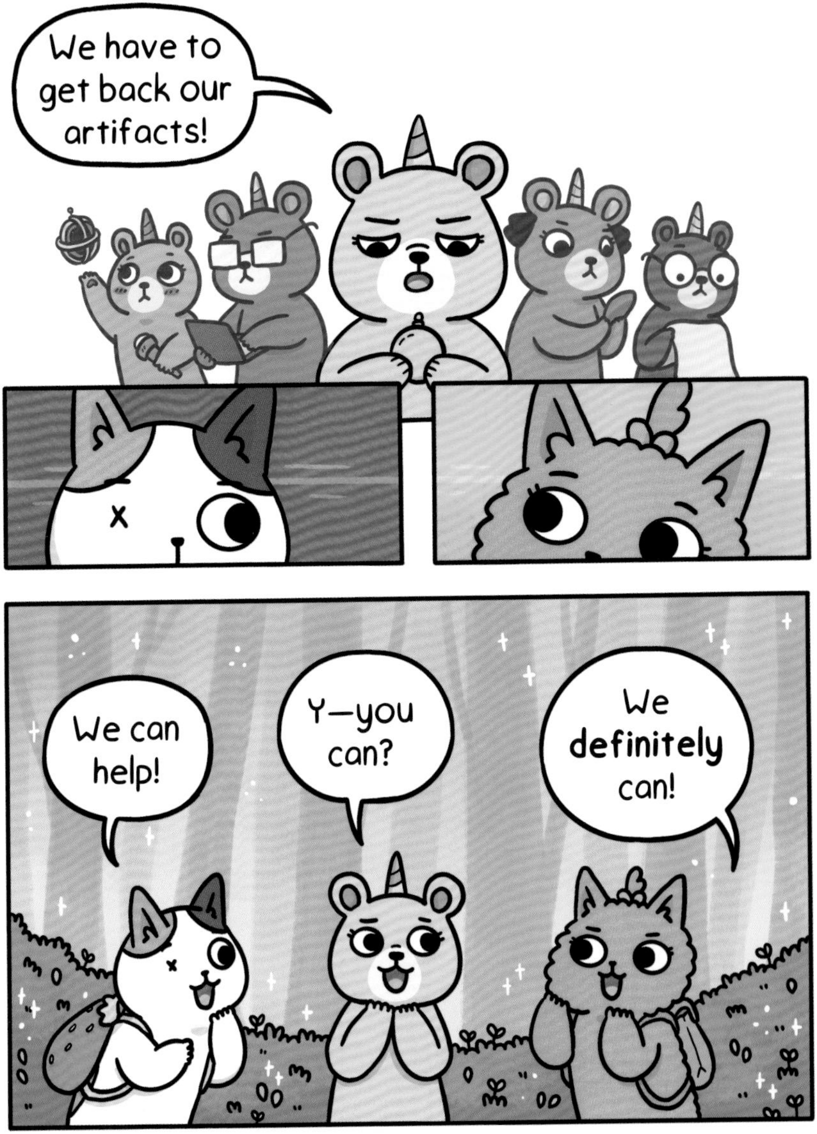
We have to get back our artifacts!
We can help!
Y—you can?
We **definitely** can!

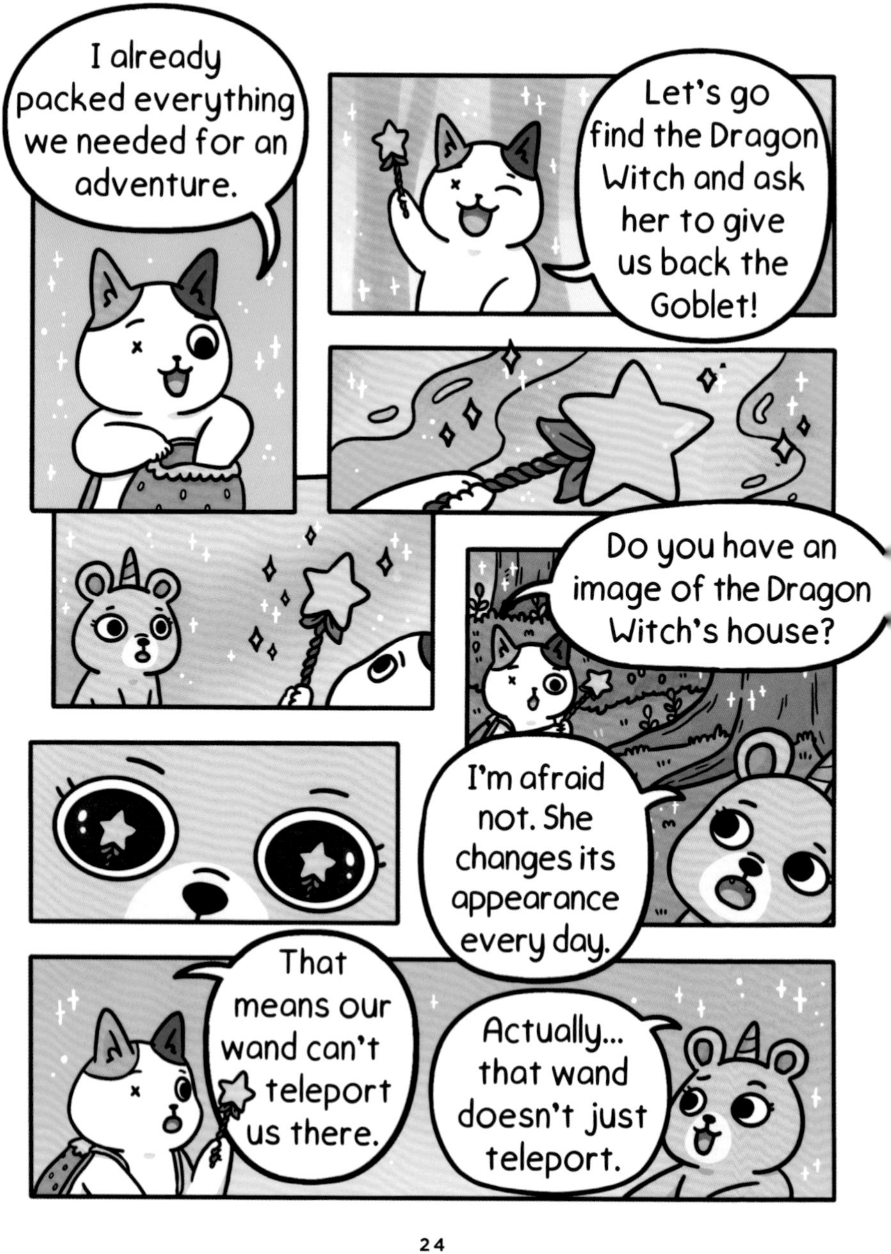
I already packed everything we needed for an adventure.
Let's go find the Dragon Witch and ask her to give us back the Goblet!
Do you have an image of the Dragon Witch's house?
I'm afraid not. She changes its appearance every day.
That means our wand can't teleport us there.
Actually... that wand doesn't just teleport.

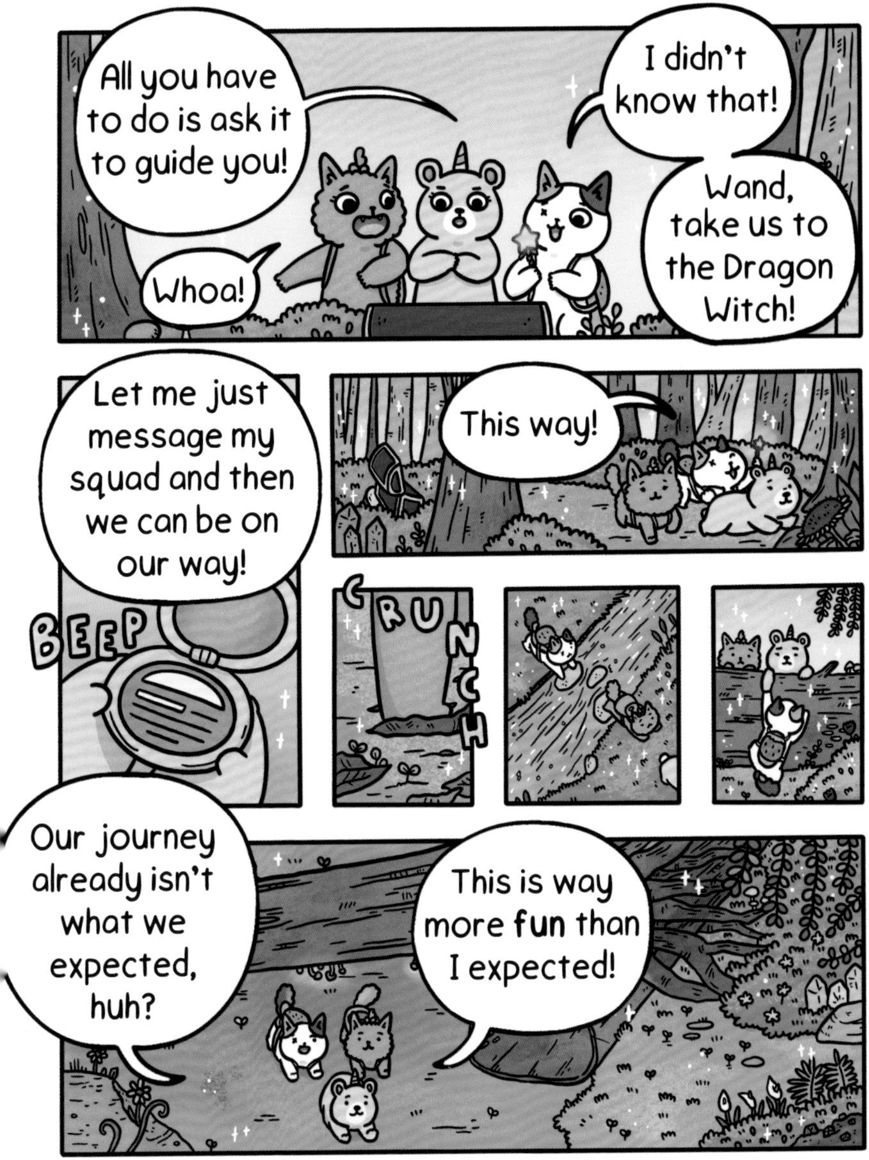
All you have to do is ask it to guide you!
Whoa!
I didn't know that!
Wand, take us to the Dragon Witch!
Let me just message my squad and then we can be on our way!
BEEP
This way!
CRUNCH
Our journey already isn't what we expected, huh?
This is way more **fun** than I expected!

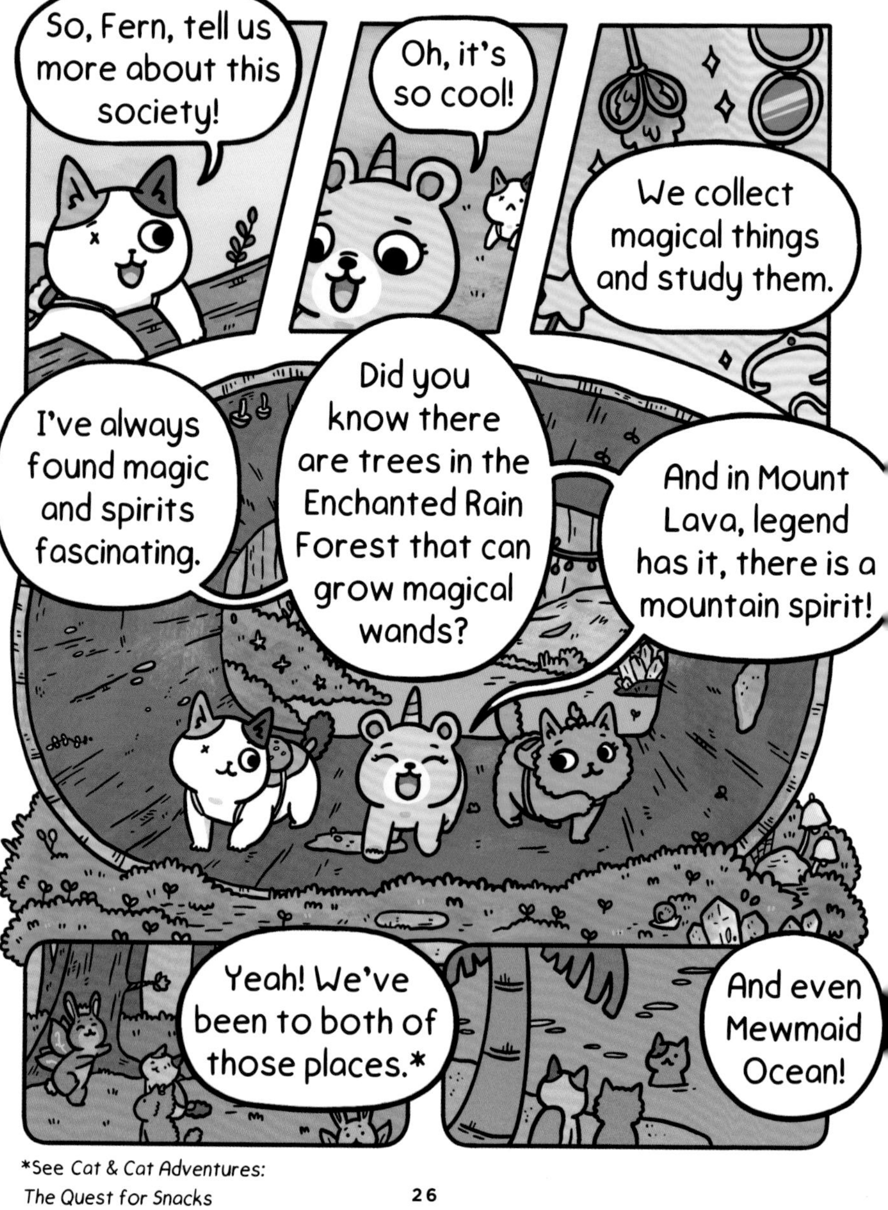
So, Fern, tell us more about this society!
Oh, it's so cool!
We collect magical things and study them.
I've always found magic and spirits fascinating.
Did you know there are trees in the Enchanted Rain Forest that can grow magical wands?
And in Mount Lava, legend has it, there is a mountain spirit!
Yeah! We've been to both of those places.*
And even Mewmaid Ocean!

*See *Cat & Cat Adventures: The Quest for Snacks*

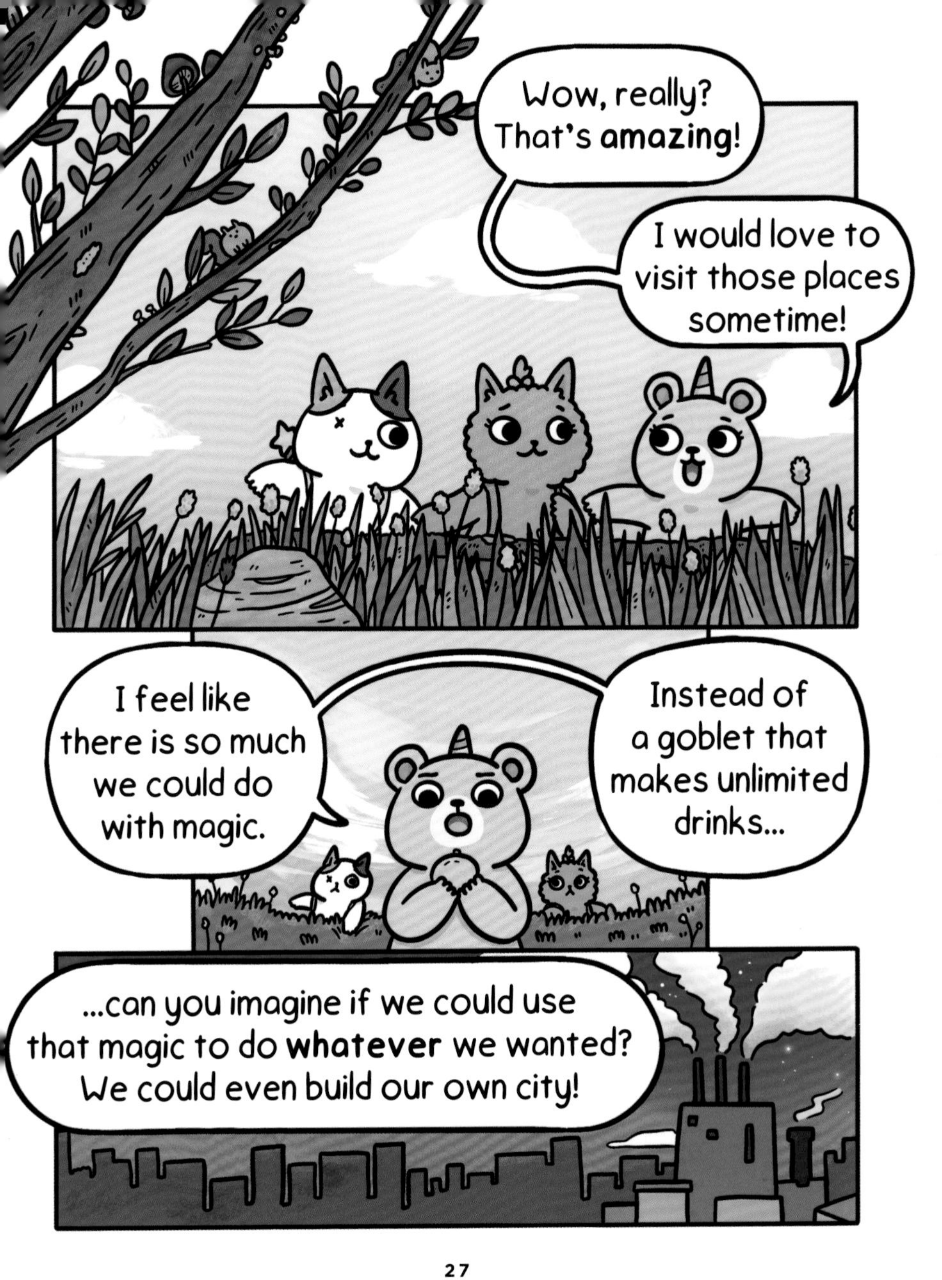
Wow, really? That's **amazing**!
I would love to visit those places sometime!
I feel like there is so much we could do with magic.
Instead of a goblet that makes unlimited drinks...
...can you imagine if we could use that magic to do **whatever** we wanted? We could even build our own city!

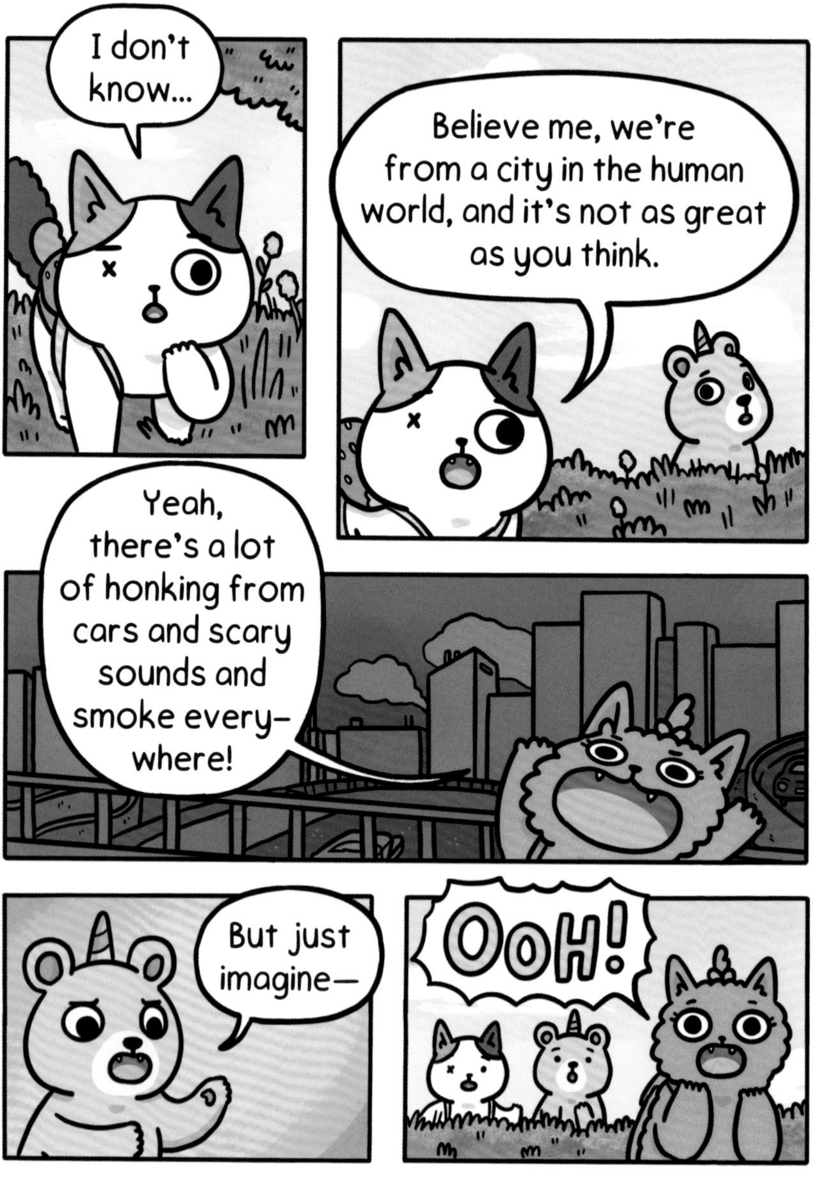
I don't know...
Believe me, we're from a city in the human world, and it's not as great as you think.
Yeah, there's a lot of honking from cars and scary sounds and smoke every-where!
But just imagine—
OOH!

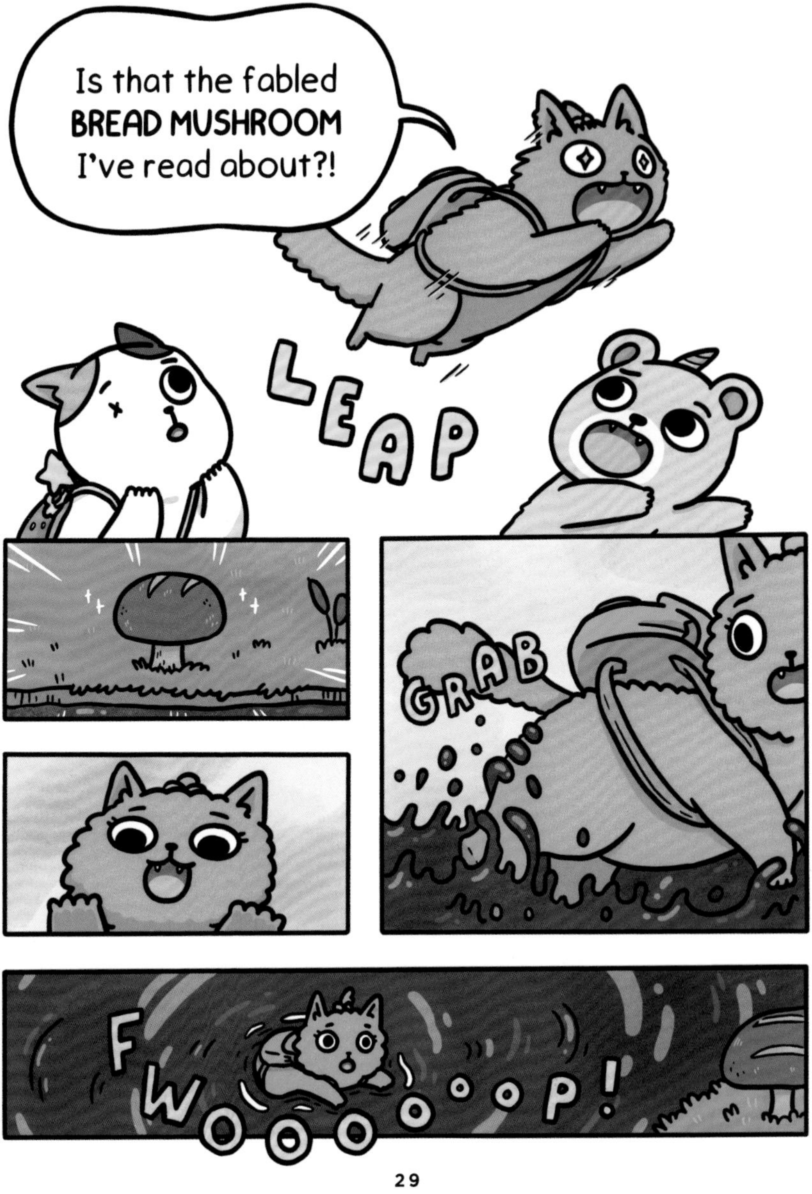
Is that the fabled BREAD MUSHROOM I've read about?!
LEAP
GRAB
FWOOOOOOOP!

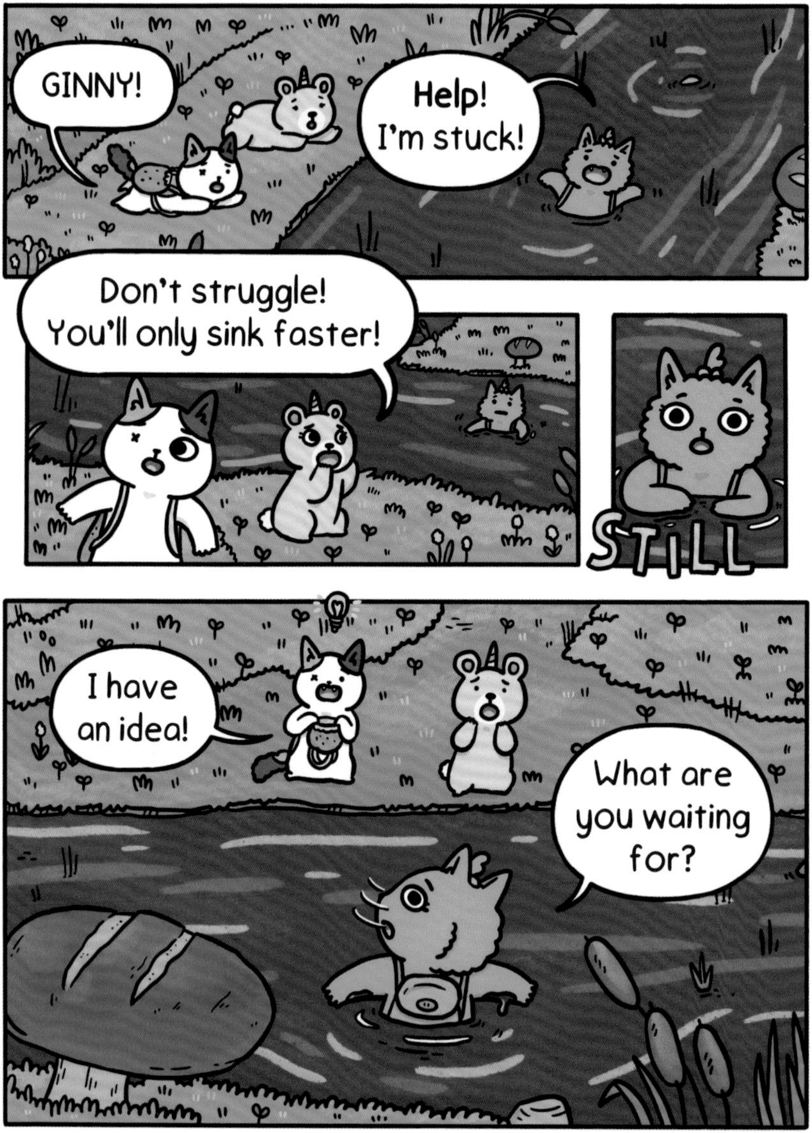
GINNY!
Help! I'm stuck!
Don't struggle! You'll only sink faster!
STILL
I have an idea!
What are you waiting for?

CHAPTER THREE: King Bum Bum

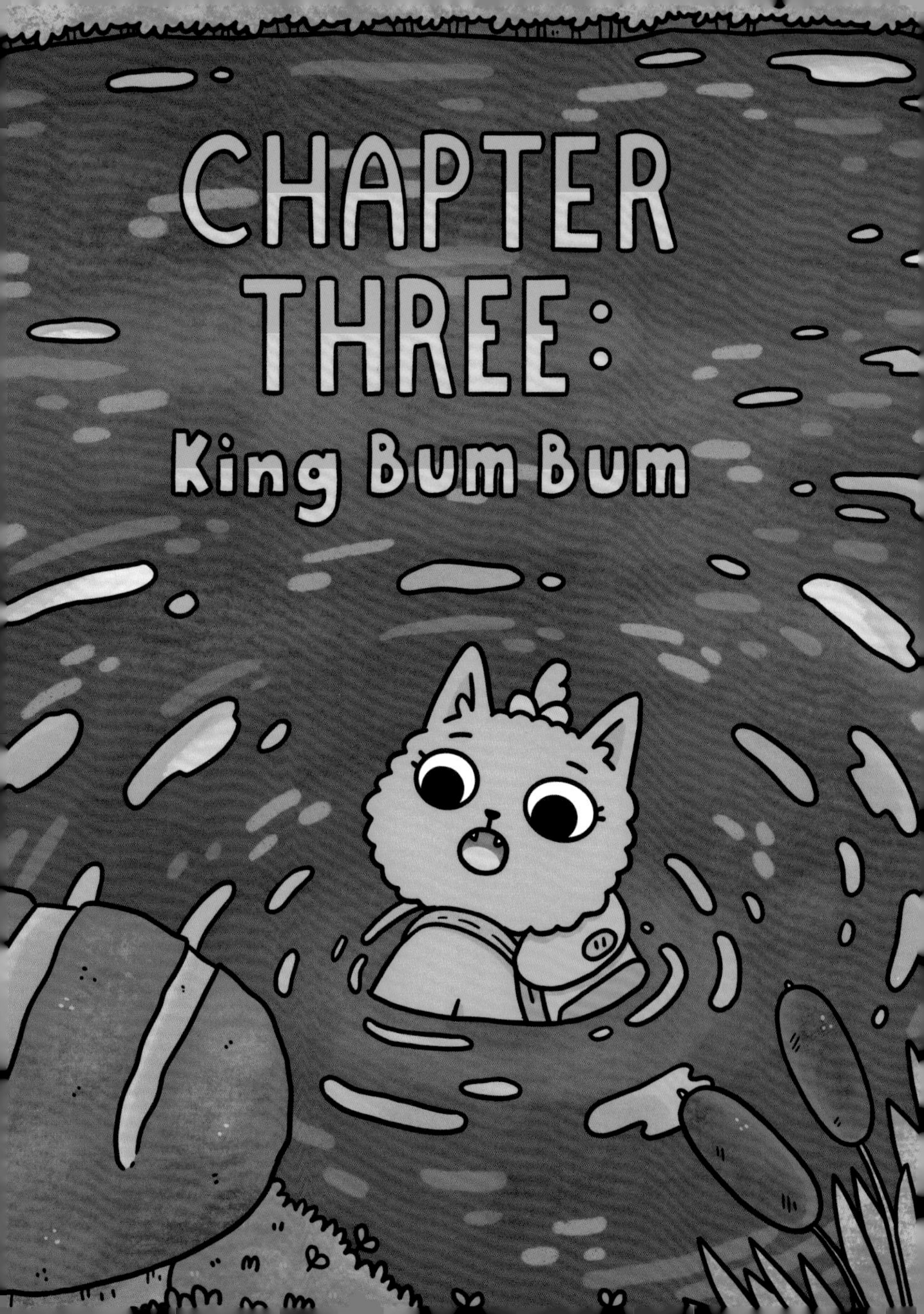

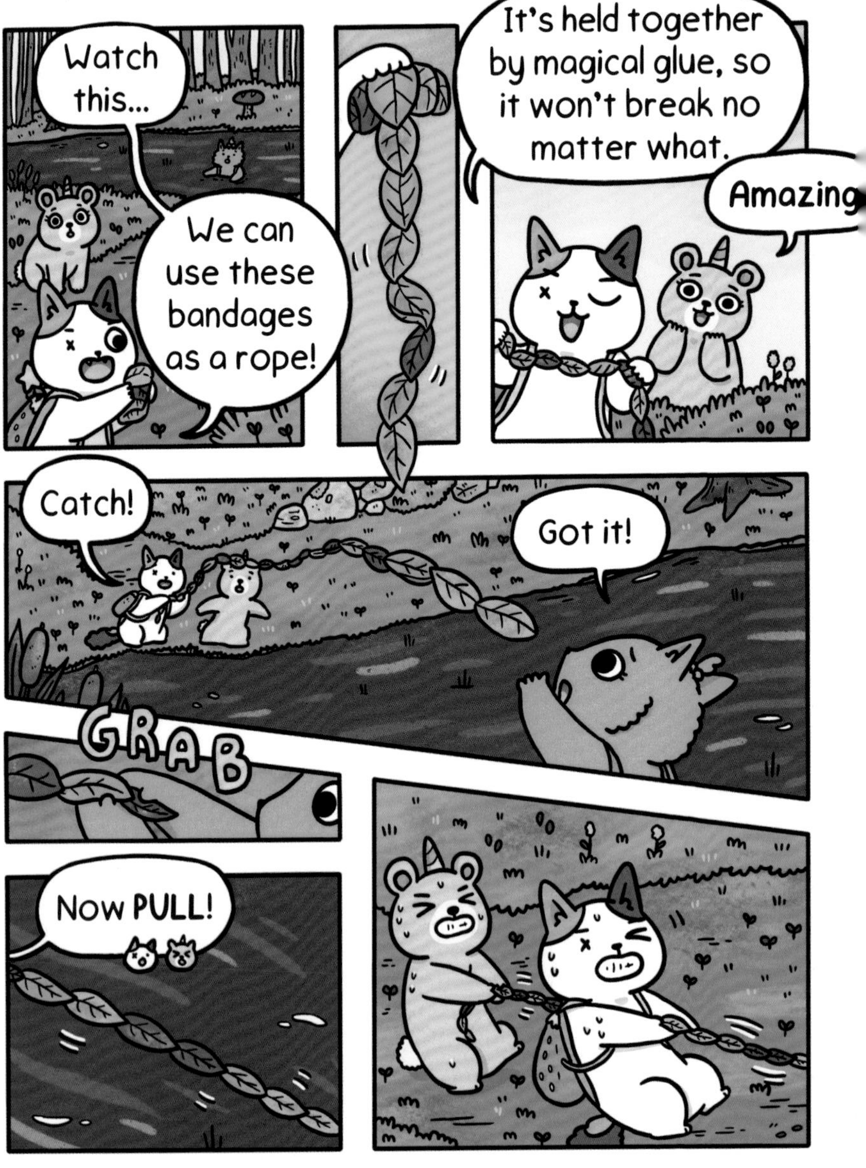

Watch this...
We can use these bandages as a rope!
It's held together by magical glue, so it won't break no matter what.
Amazing
Catch!
Got it!
GRAB
Now PULL!

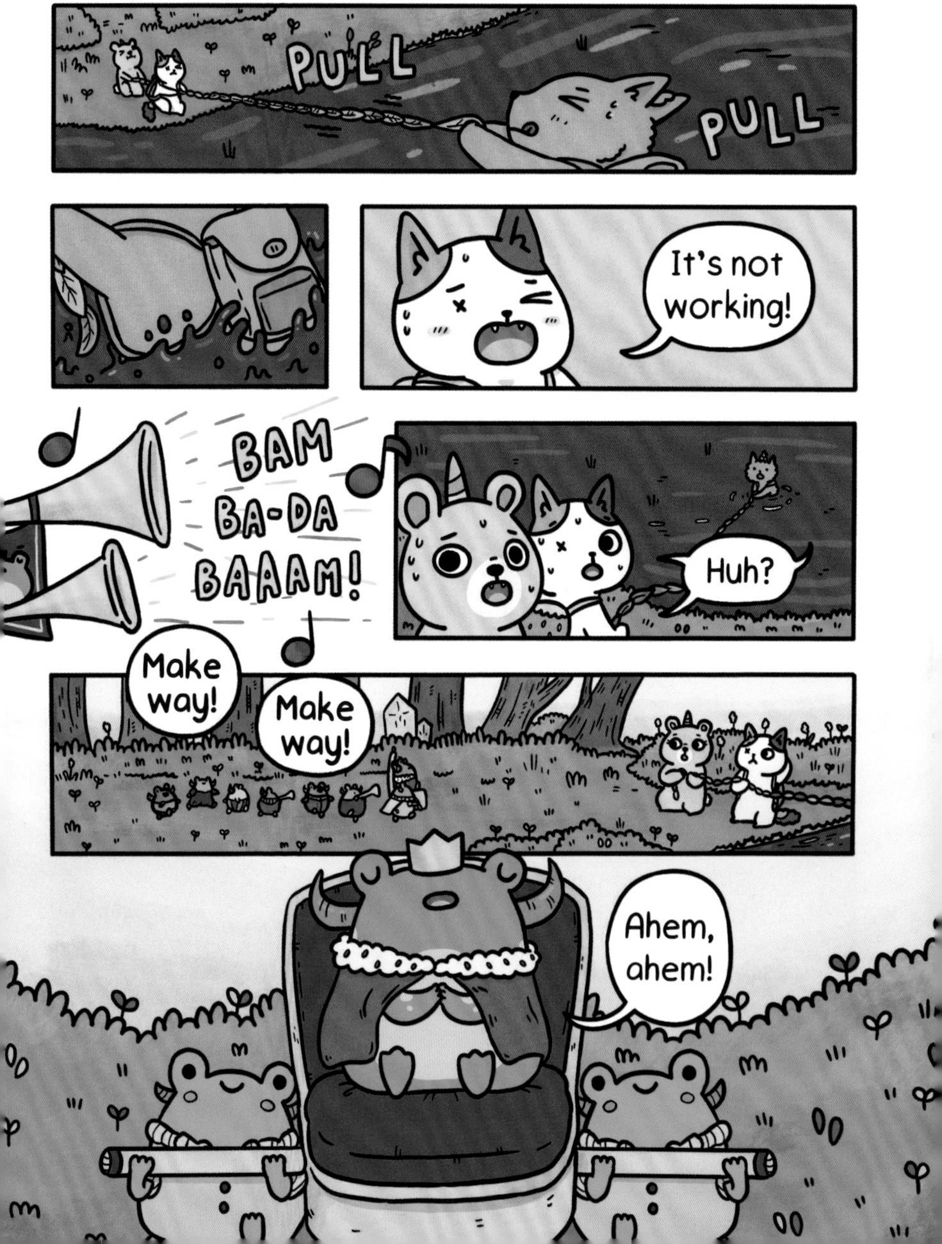
PULL
PULL
It's not working!
BAM BA-DA BAAAM!
Huh?
Make way!
Make way!
Ahem, ahem!

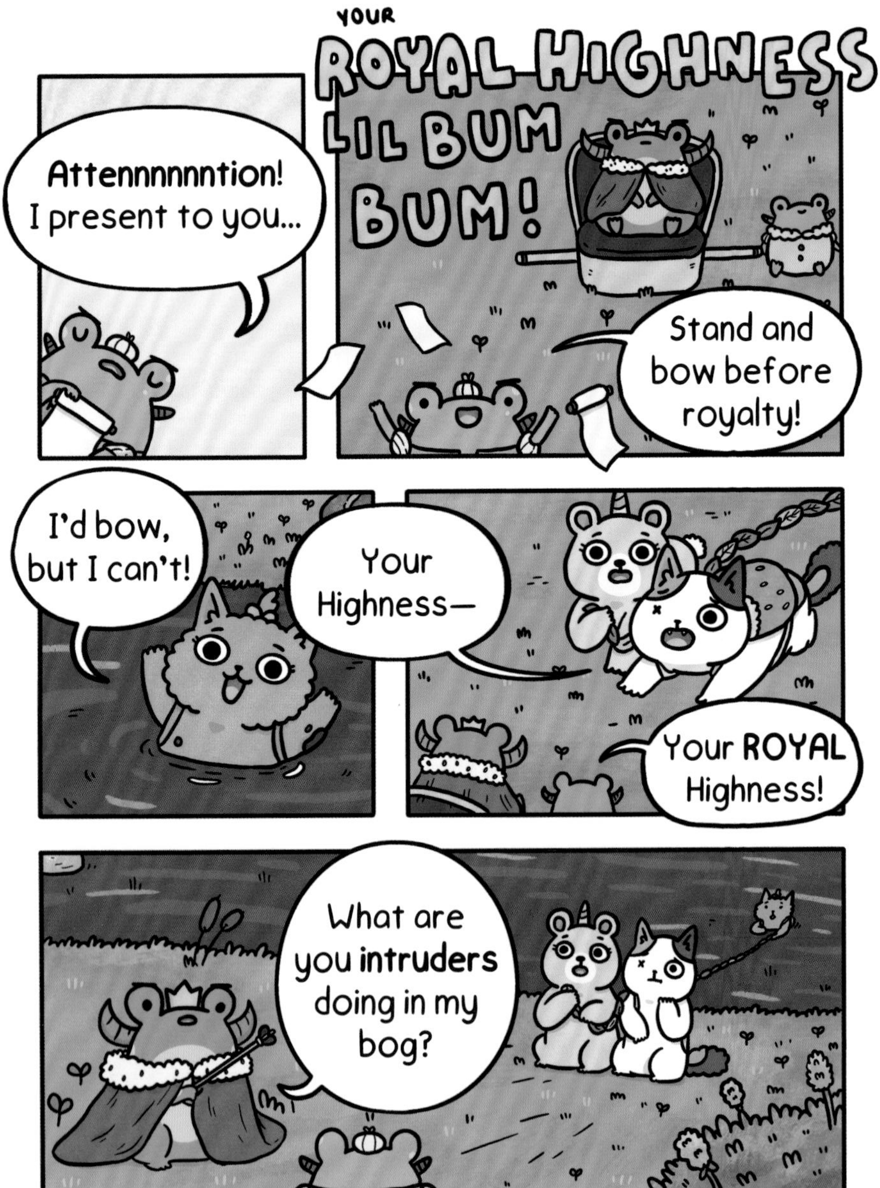
Attennnnnntion! I present to you...
YOUR ROYAL HIGHNESS LIL BUM BUM!
Stand and bow before royalty!
I'd bow, but I can't!
Your Highness—
Your ROYAL Highness!
What are you intruders doing in my bog?

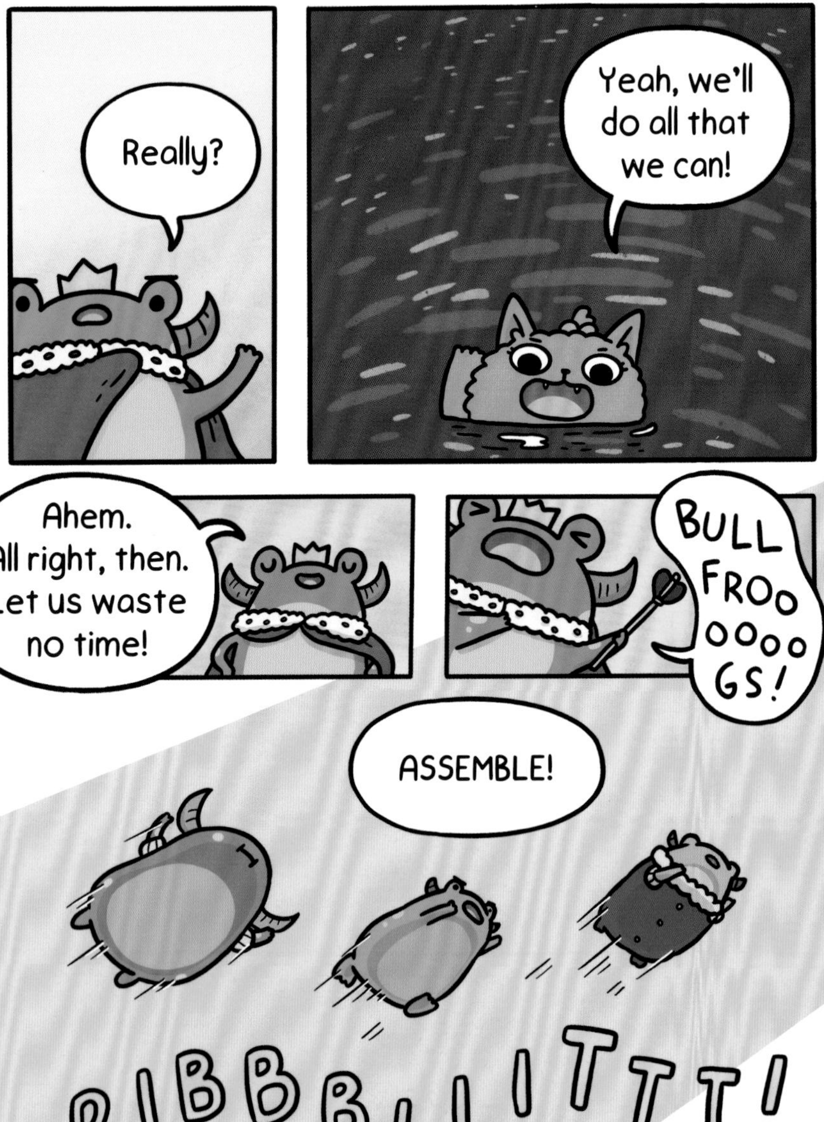

Really?
Yeah, we'll do all that we can!
Ahem. All right, then. Let us waste no time!
BULL FROOOOOOGS!
ASSEMBLE!
RIBBBIIITTTT!

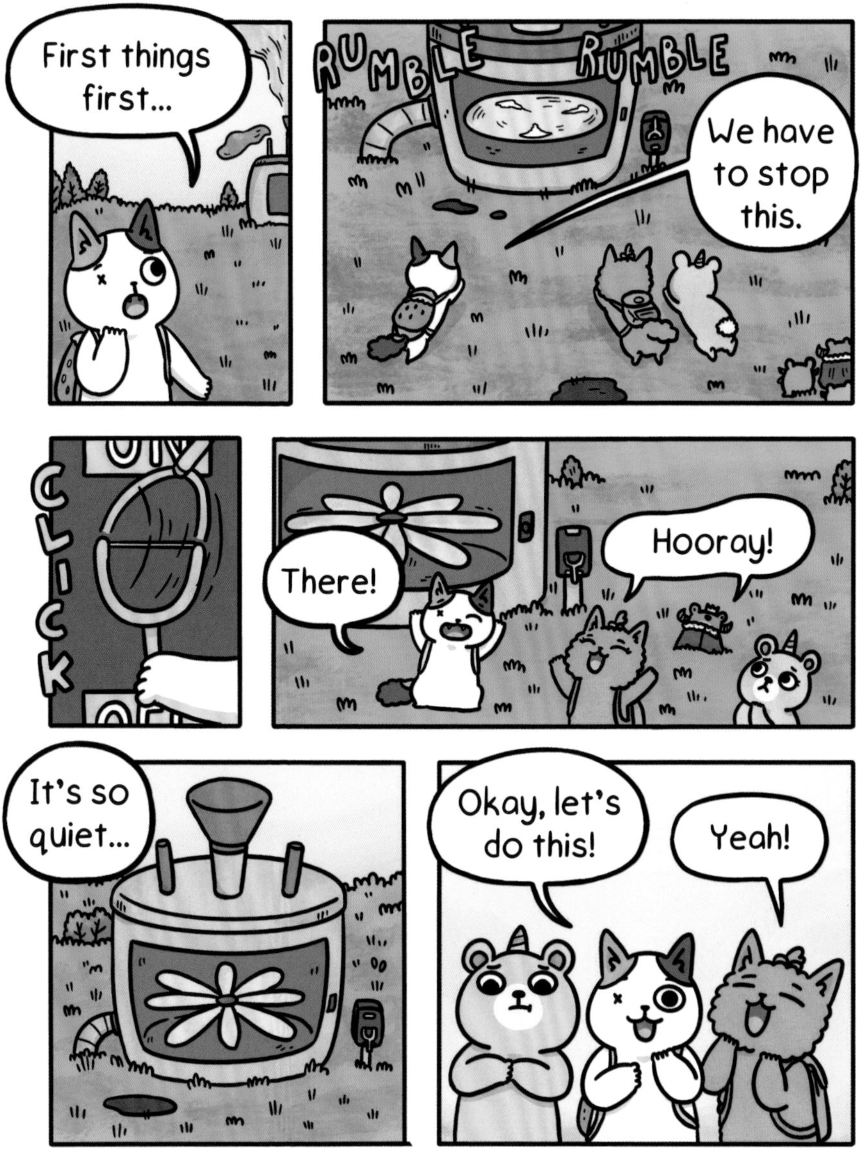
First things first...
RUMBLE RUMBLE
We have to stop this.
CLICK
There!
Hooray!
It's so quiet...
Okay, let's do this!
Yeah!

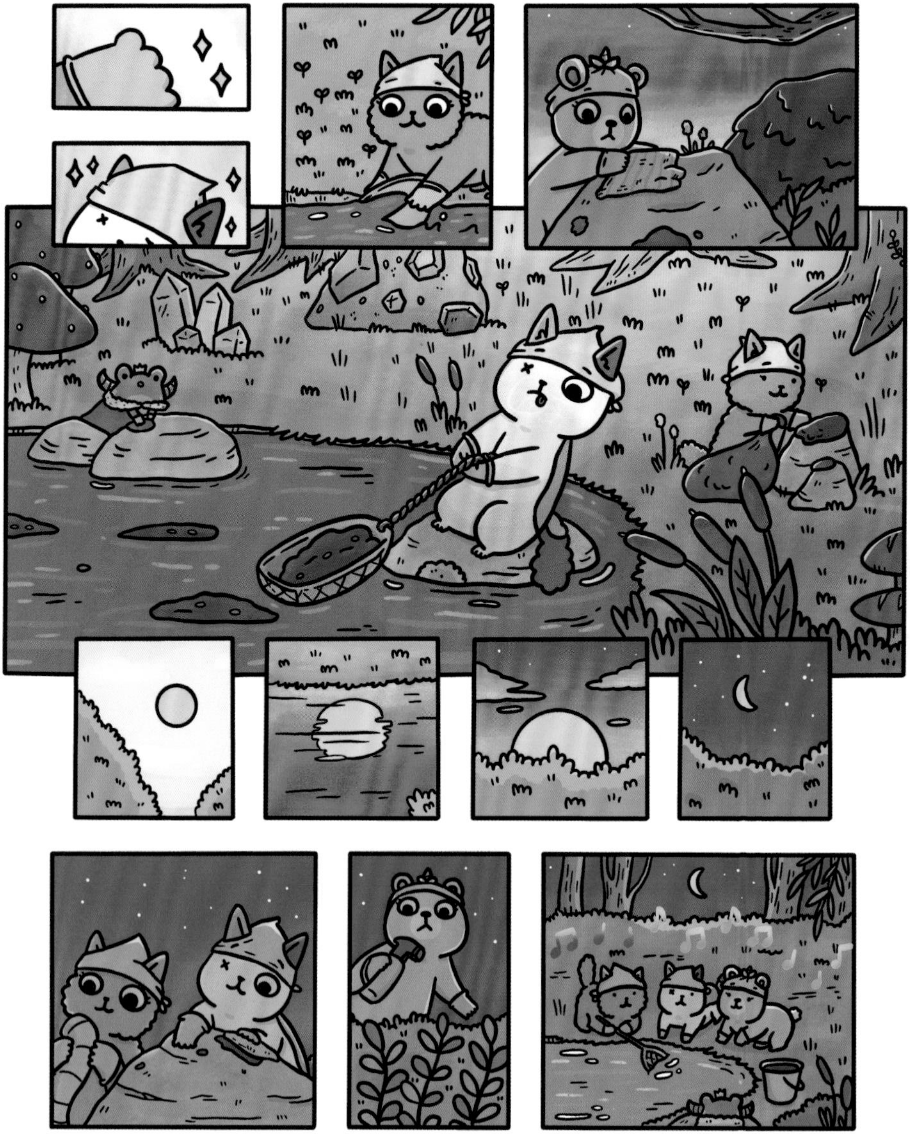

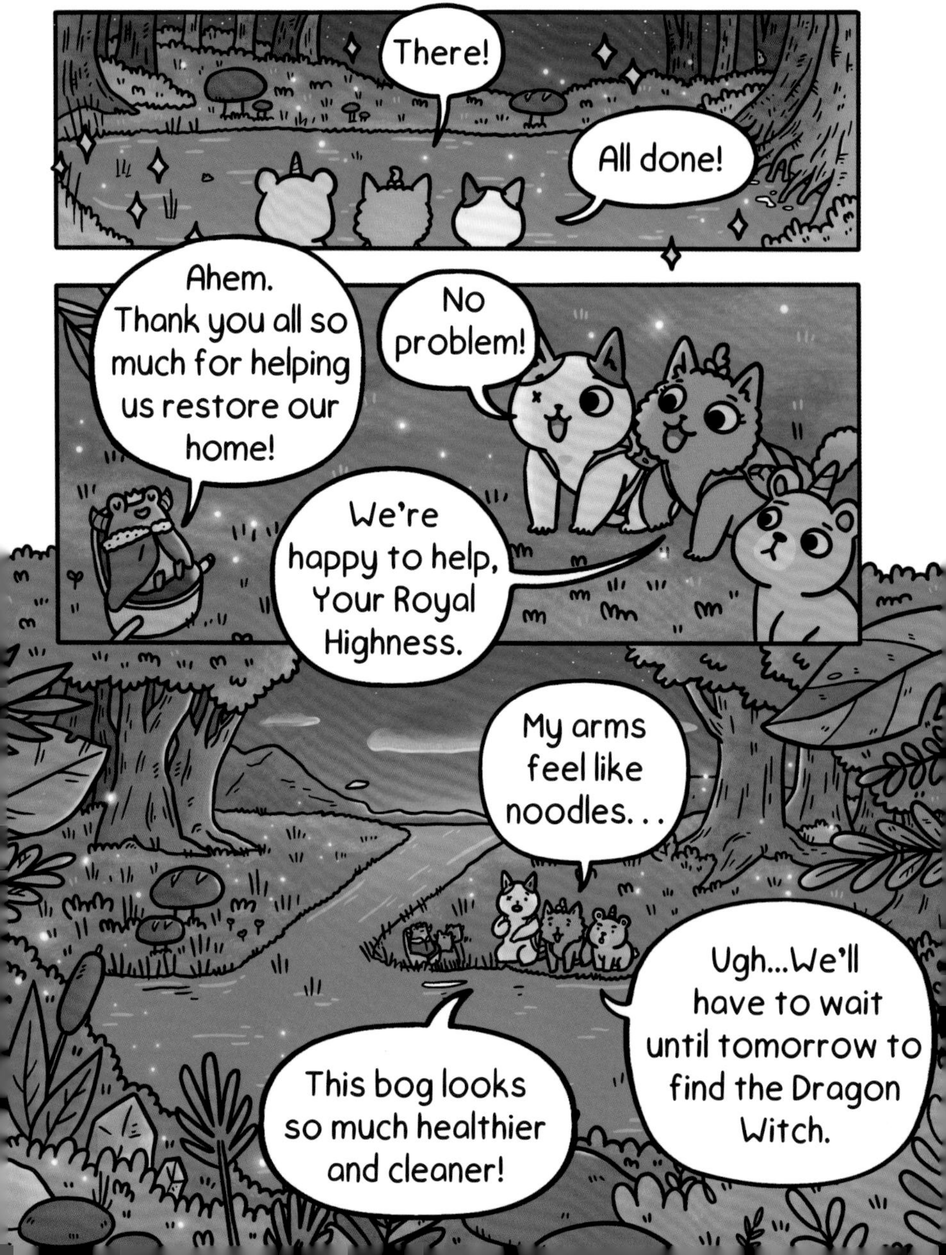
There!
All done!
Ahem. Thank you all so much for helping us restore our home!
No problem!
We're happy to help, Your Royal Highness.
My arms feel like noodles. . .
This bog looks so much healthier and cleaner!
Ugh...We'll have to wait until tomorrow to find the Dragon Witch.

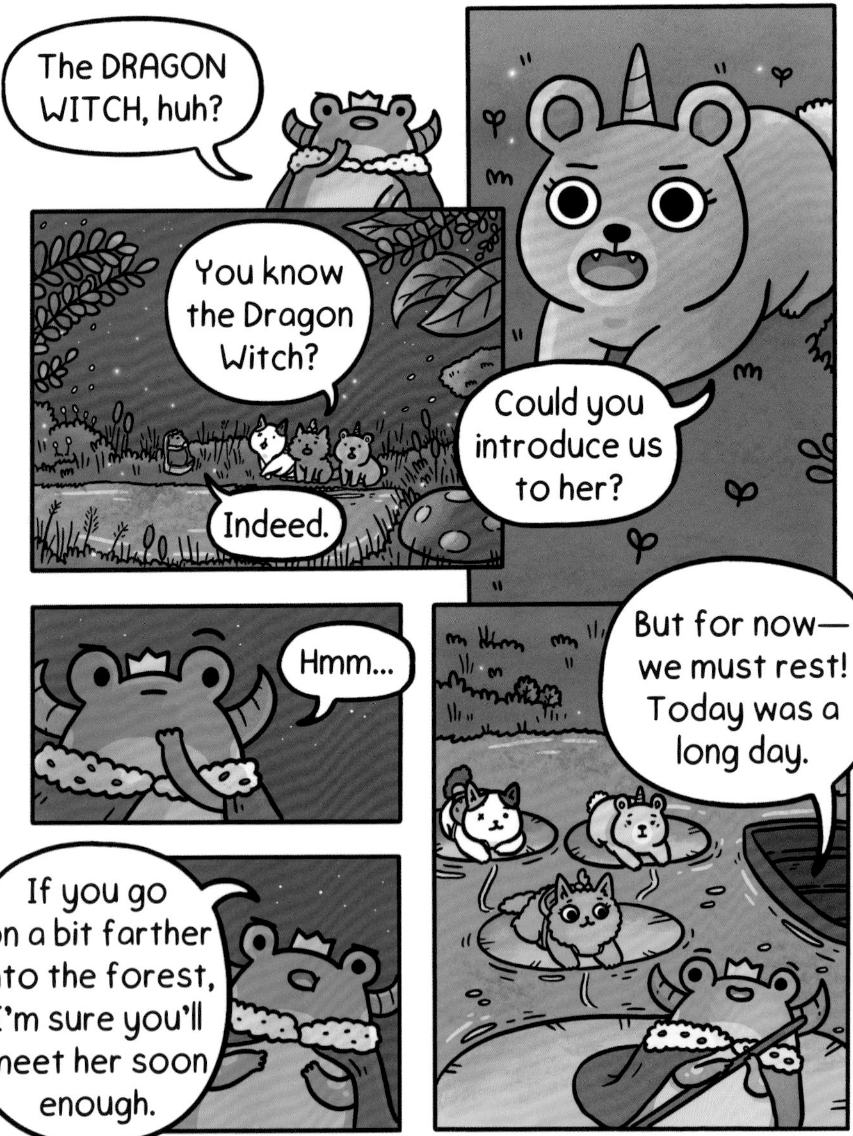
The DRAGON WITCH, huh?
You know the Dragon Witch?
Indeed.
Could you introduce us to her?
Hmm...
If you go on a bit farther into the forest, I'm sure you'll meet her soon enough.
But for now— we must rest! Today was a long day.

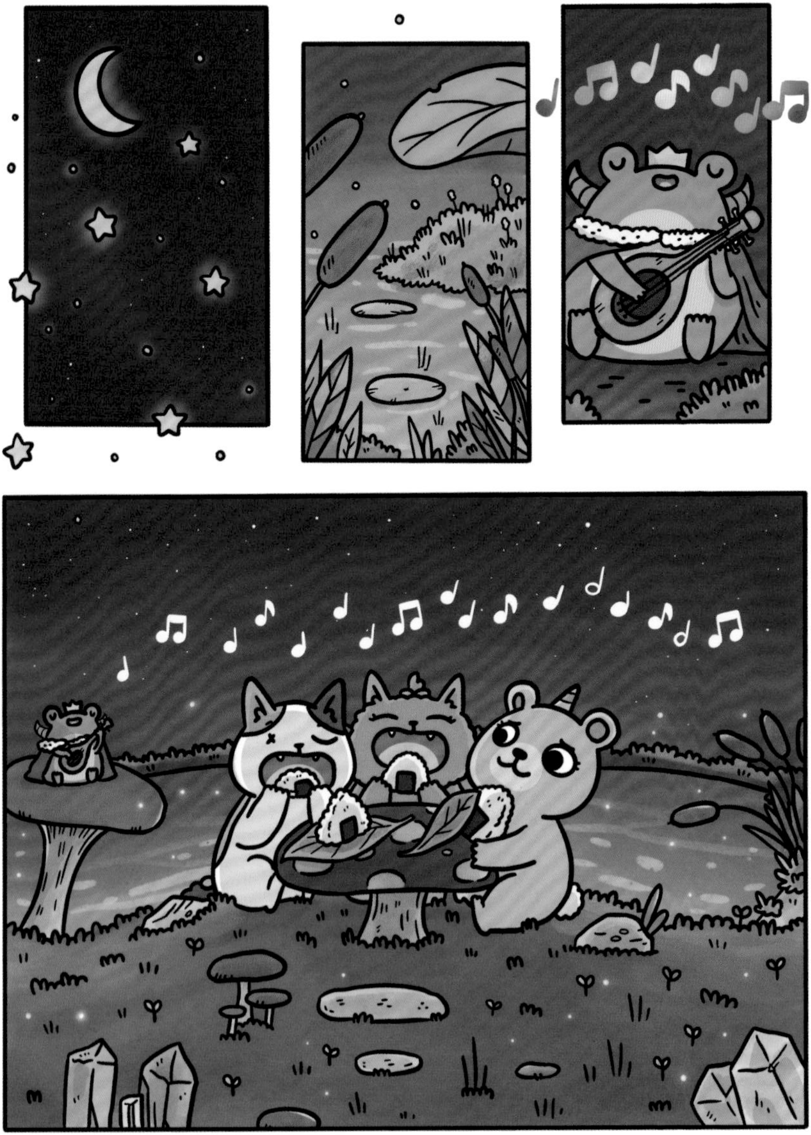

CHAPTER FOUR:

Cinder

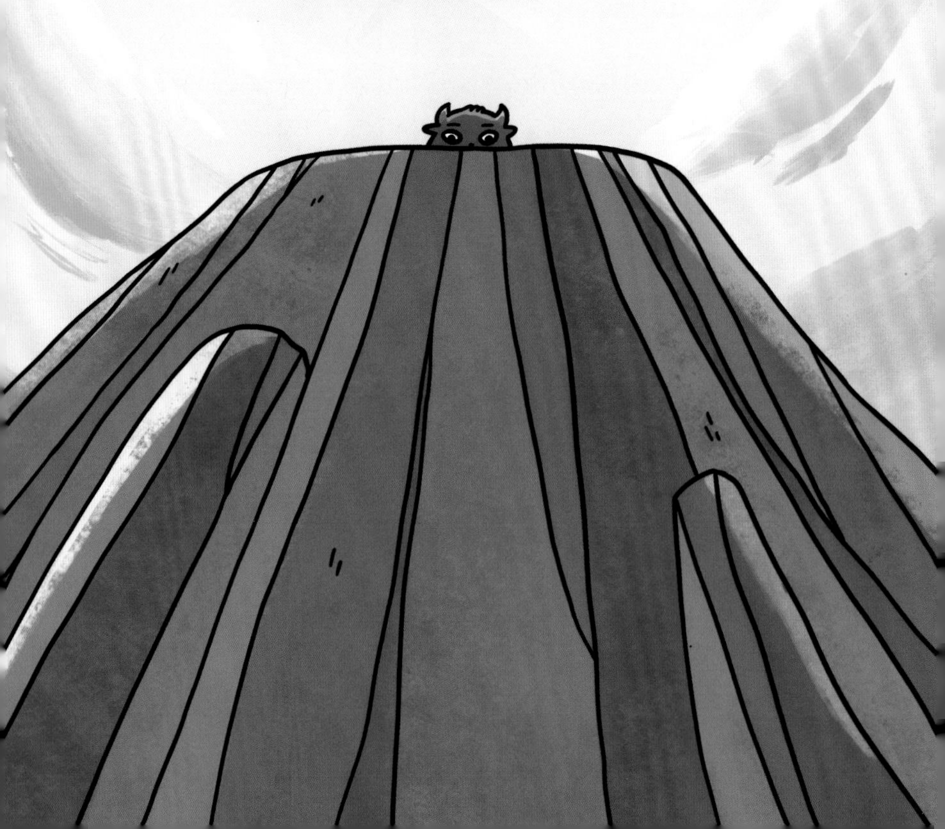

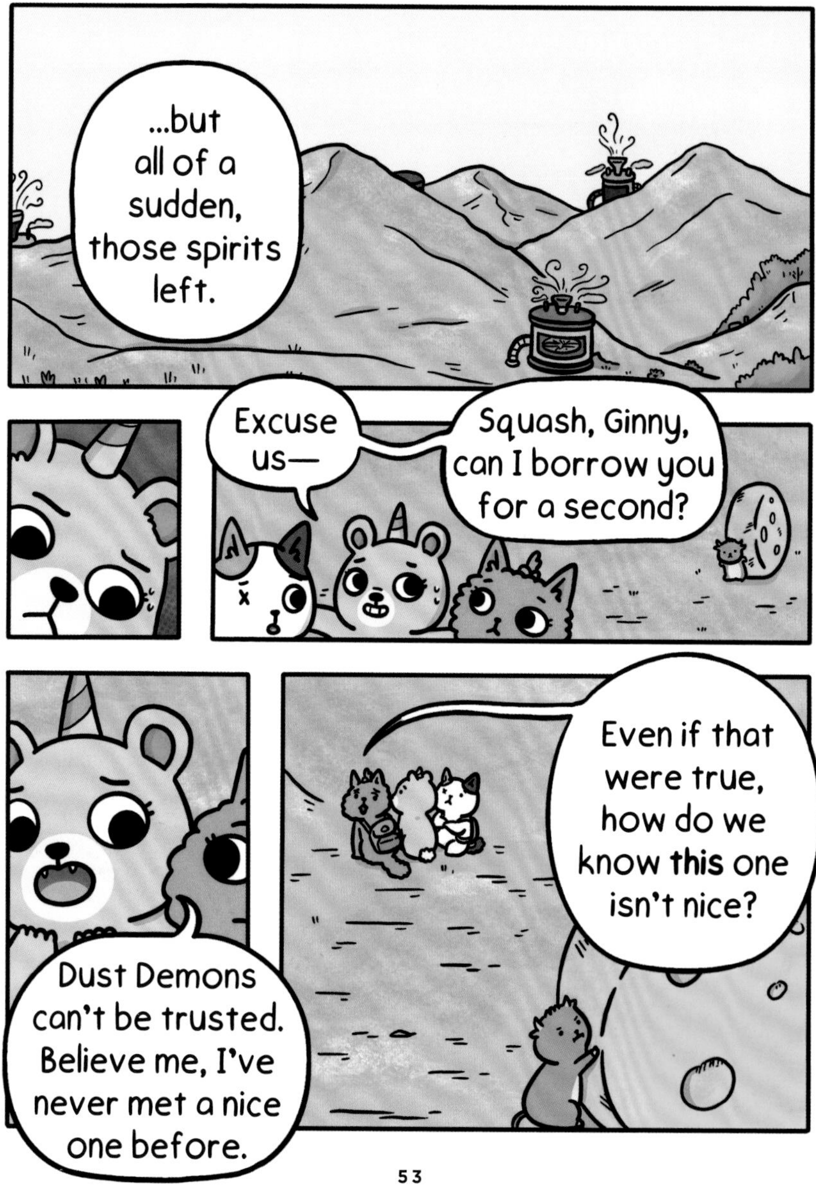
...but all of a sudden, those spirits left.
Excuse us—
Squash, Ginny, can I borrow you for a second?
Dust Demons can't be trusted. Believe me, I've never met a nice one before.
Even if that were true, how do we know **this** one isn't nice?

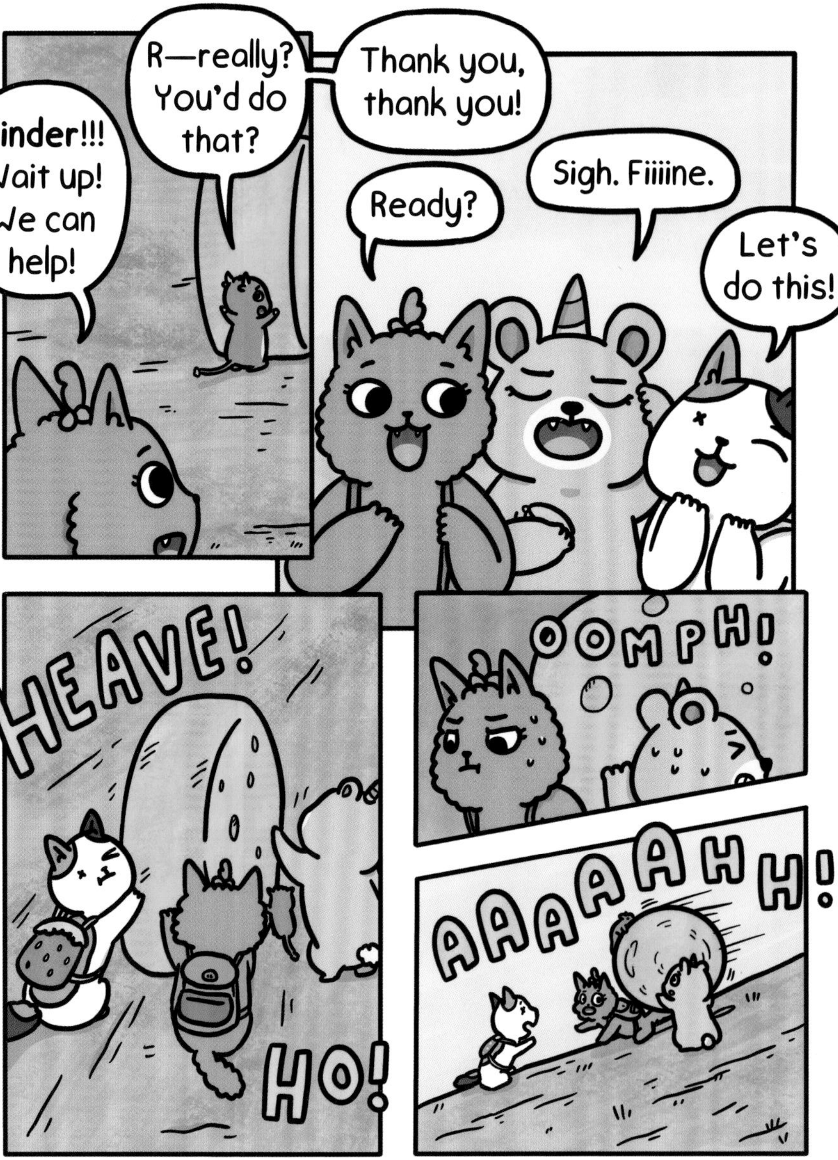
Cinder!!! Wait up! We can help!
R—really? You'd do that?
Thank you, thank you!
Ready?
Sigh. Fiiiine.
Let's do this!
HEAVE!
HO!
OOMPH!
AAAAAAHHH!

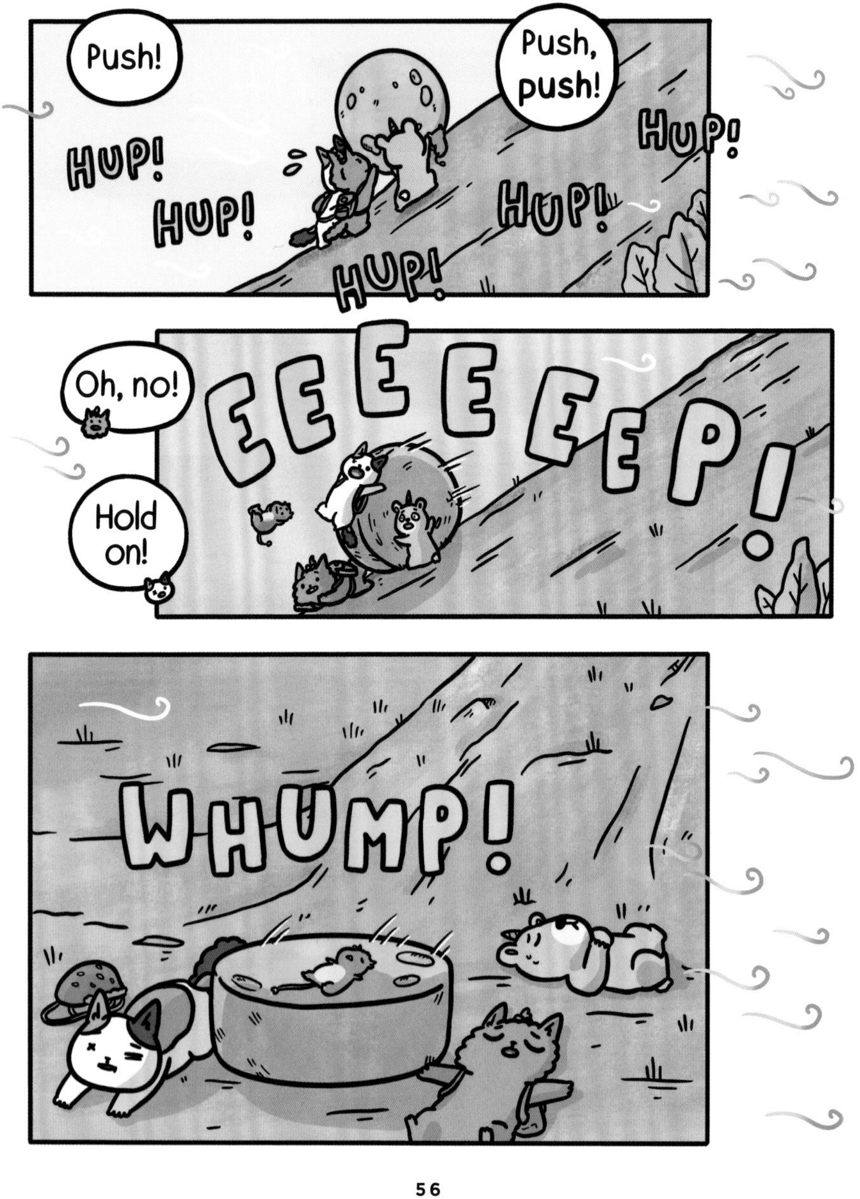
Push!
Push, push!
HUP!
HUP!
HUP!
HUP!
HUP!
Oh, no!
Hold on!
EEEEEEEP!
WHUMP!

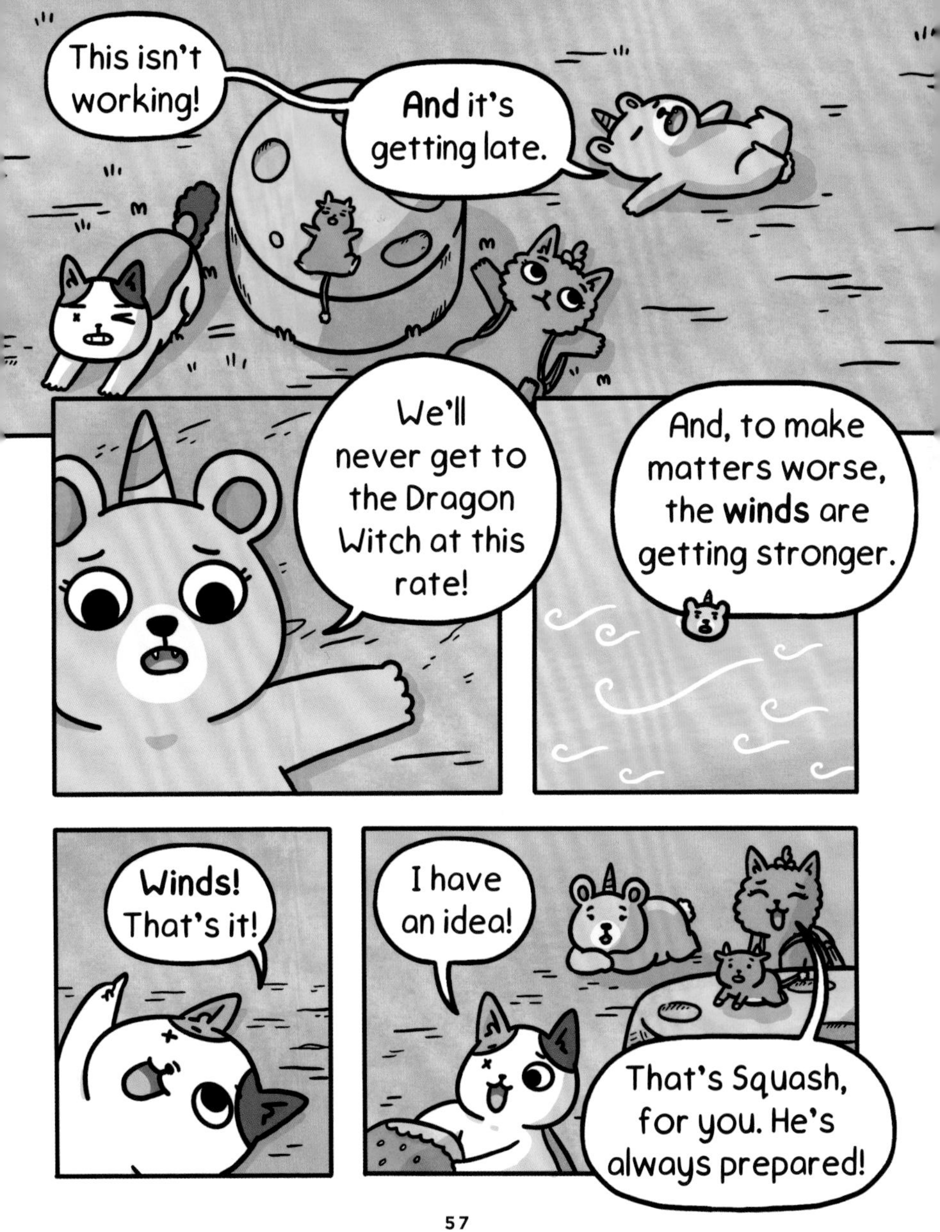
This isn't working!
And it's getting late.
We'll never get to the Dragon Witch at this rate!
And, to make matters worse, the **winds** are getting stronger.
Winds! That's it!
I have an idea!
That's Squash, for you. He's always prepared!

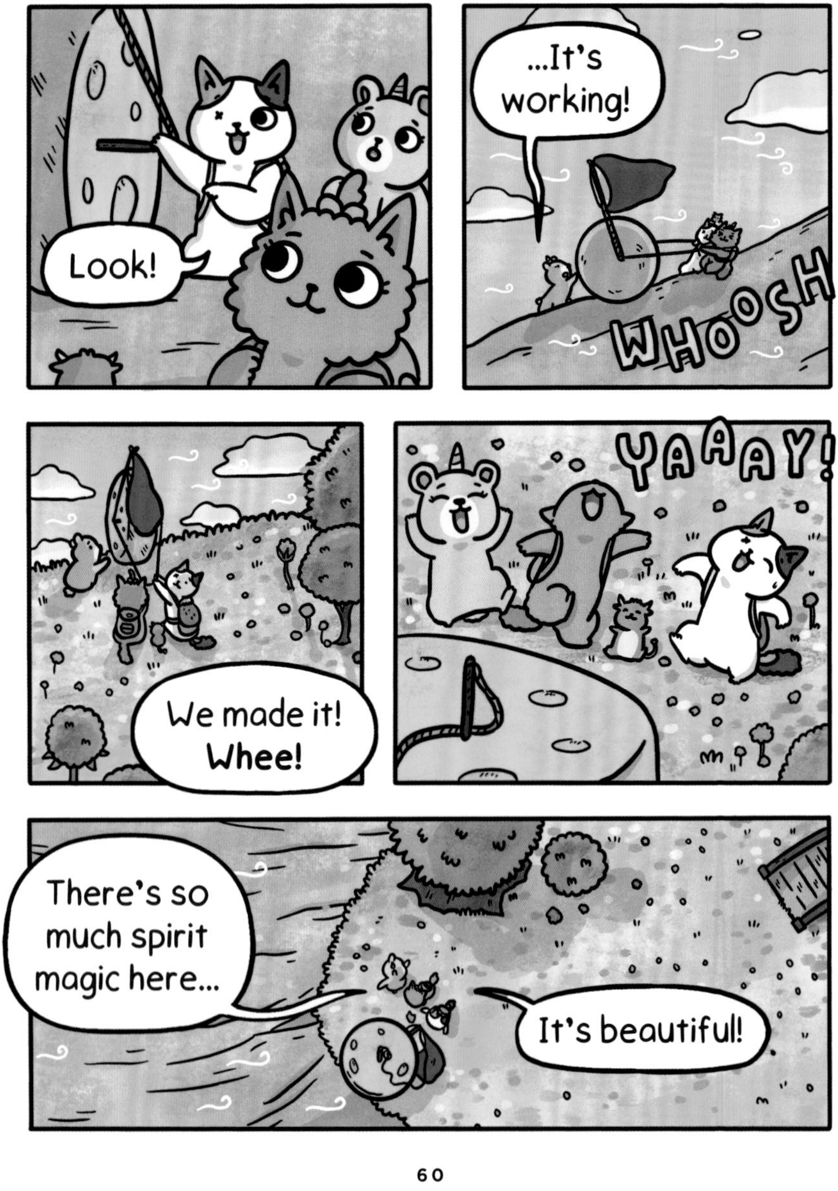
Look!
...It's working!
WHOOSH
We made it! Whee!
YAAAY!
There's so much spirit magic here...
It's beautiful!

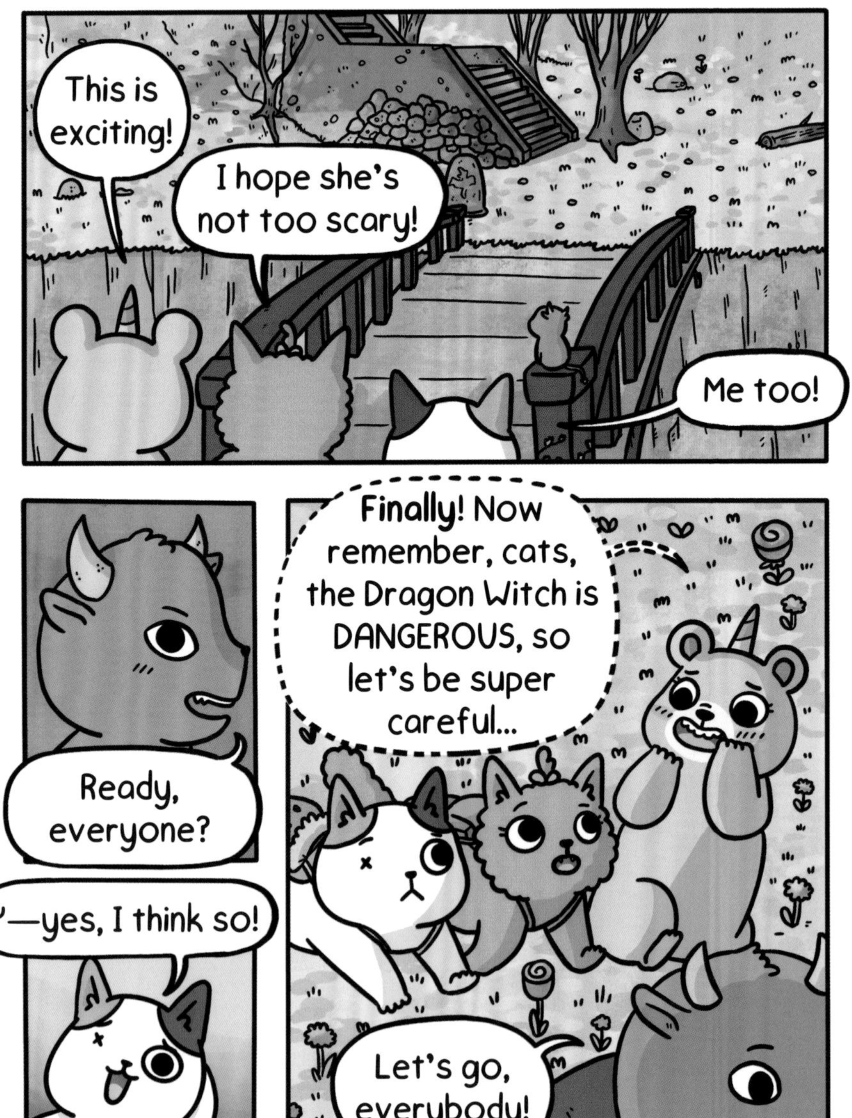
This is exciting!
I hope she's not too scary!
Me too!
Ready, everyone?
Y—yes, I think so!
Finally! Now remember, cats, the Dragon Witch is DANGEROUS, so let's be super careful...
Let's go, everybody!

CHAPTER FIVE: The Dragon Witch

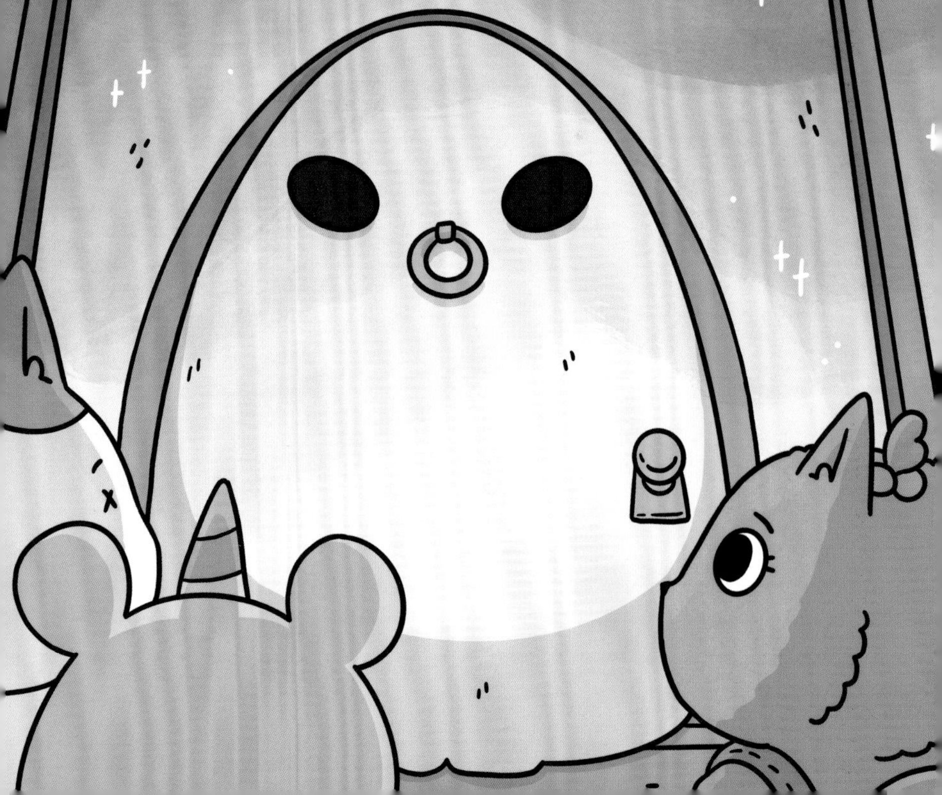

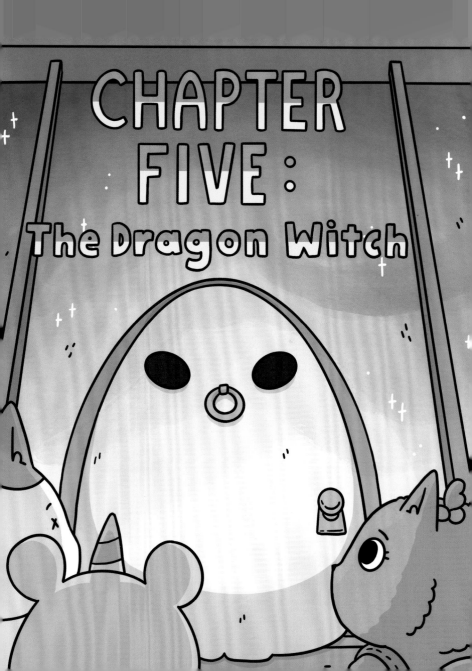

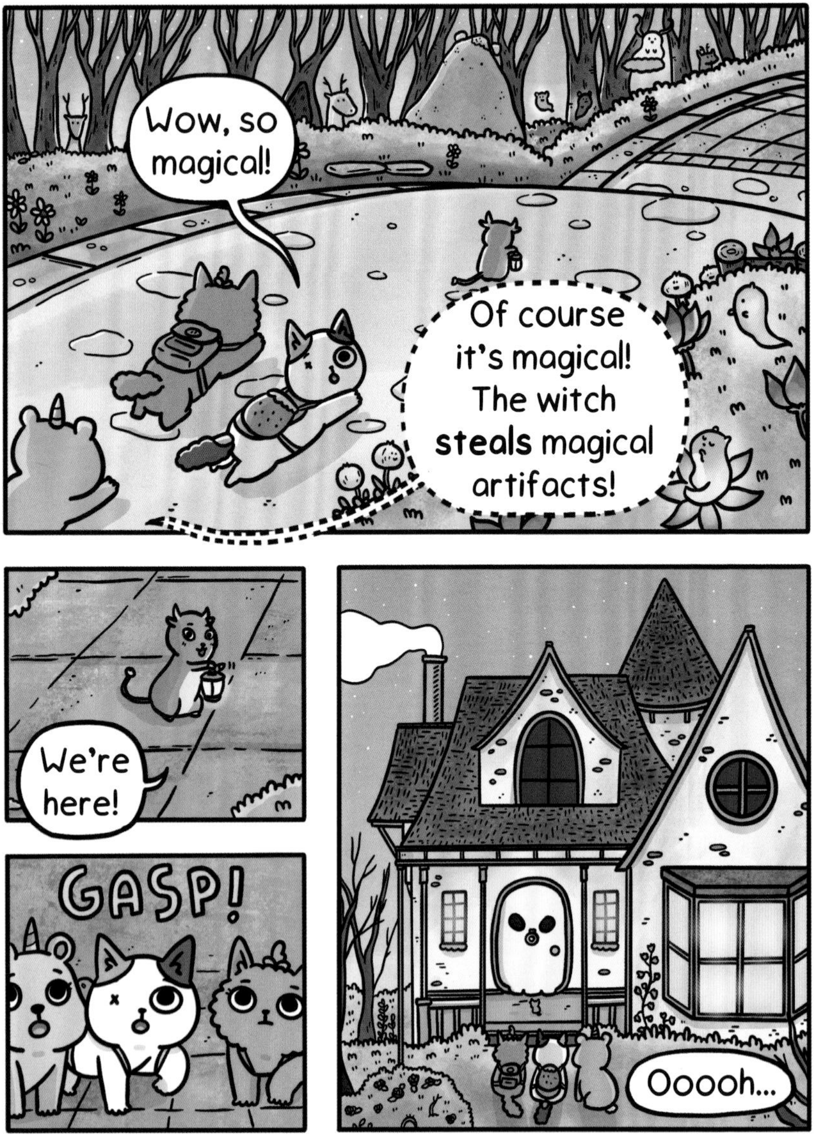
Wow, so magical!
Of course it's magical! The witch **steals** magical artifacts!
We're here!
GASP!
Ooooh...

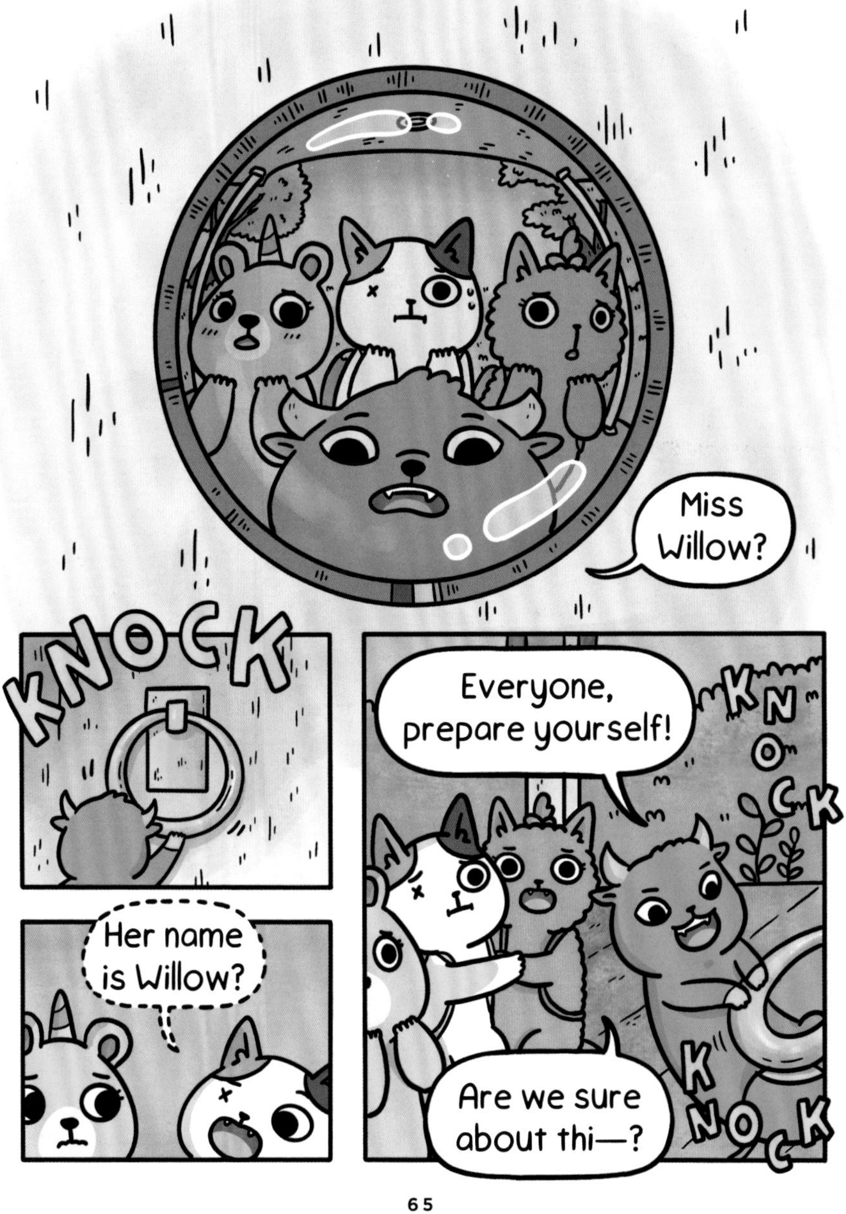
Miss Willow?
KNOCK
Her name is Willow?
Everyone, prepare yourself!
KNOCK
Are we sure about thi—?
KNOCK

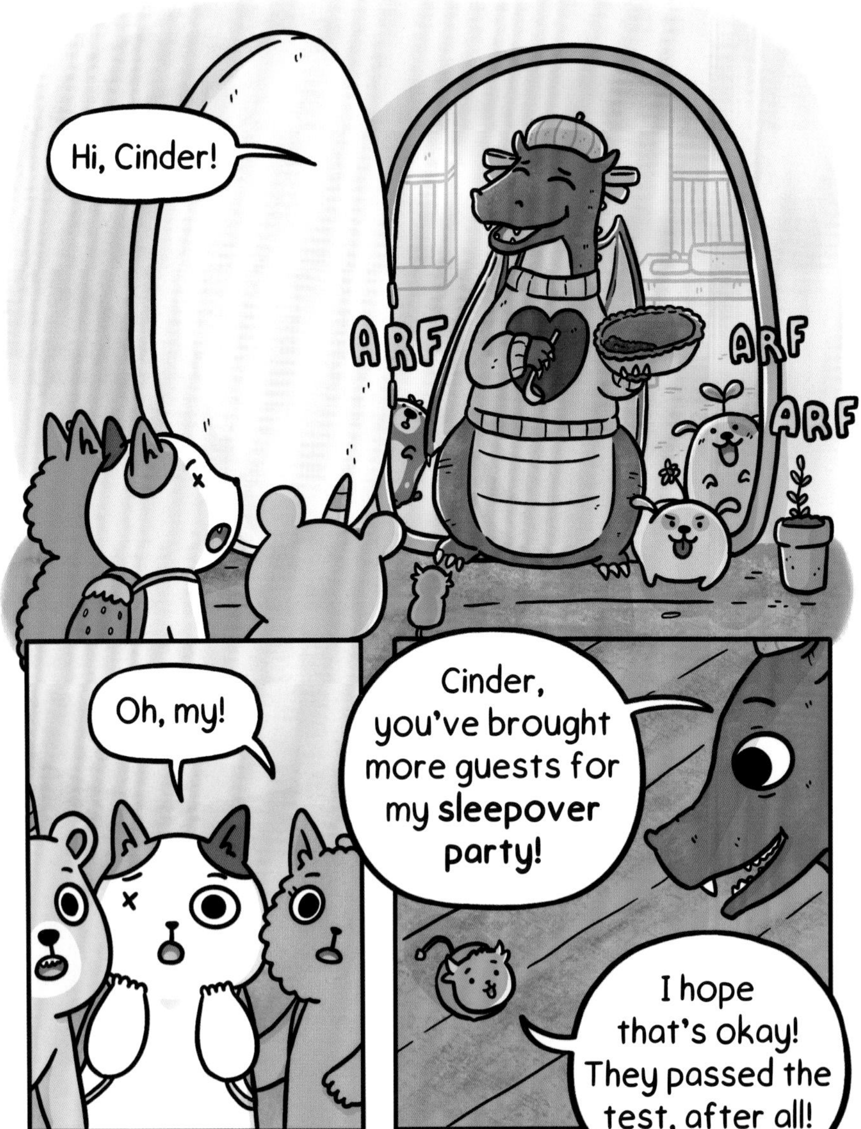
Hi, Cinder!
ARF
ARF
ARF
Oh, my!
Cinder, you've brought more guests for my **sleepover party!**
I hope that's okay! They passed the test, after all!

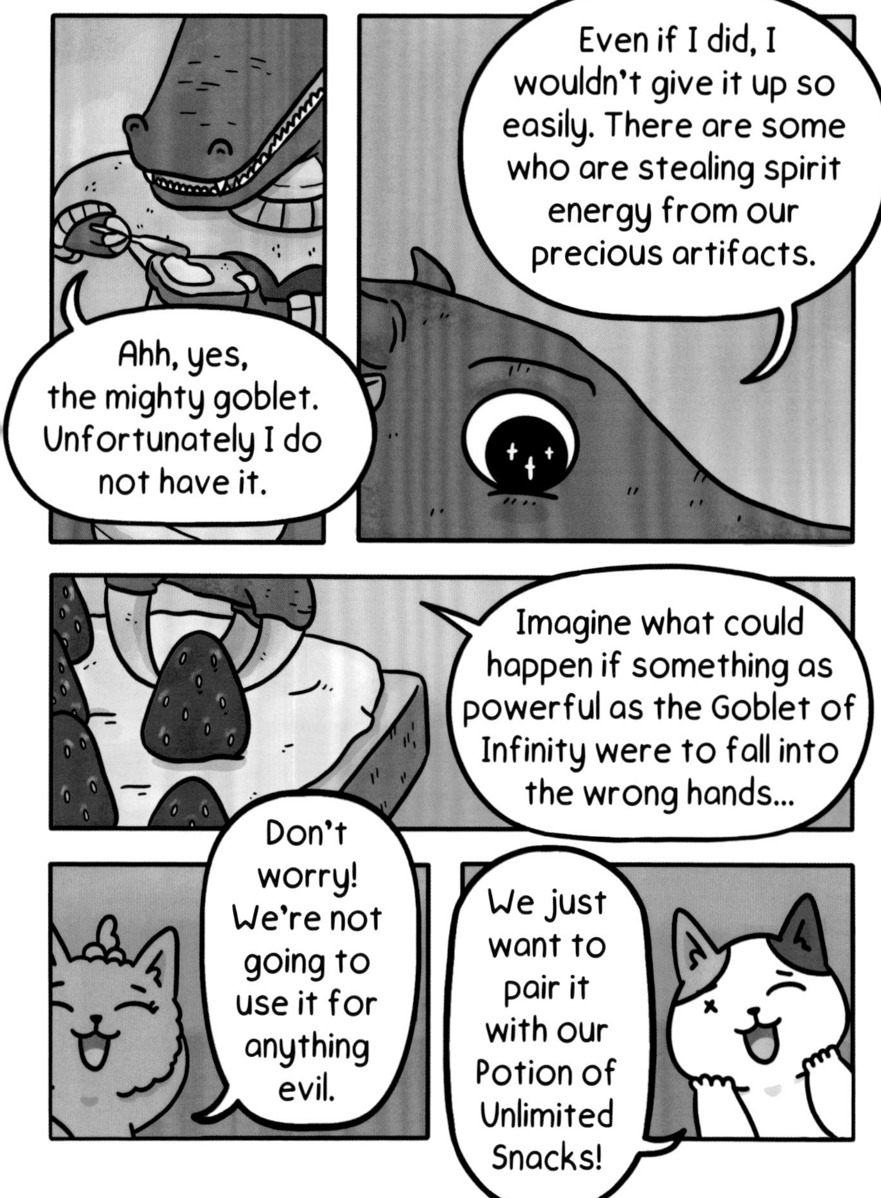
Ahh, yes, the mighty goblet. Unfortunately I do not have it.
Even if I did, I wouldn't give it up so easily. There are some who are stealing spirit energy from our precious artifacts.
Imagine what could happen if something as powerful as the Goblet of Infinity were to fall into the wrong hands...
Don't worry! We're not going to use it for anything evil.
We just want to pair it with our Potion of Unlimited Snacks!

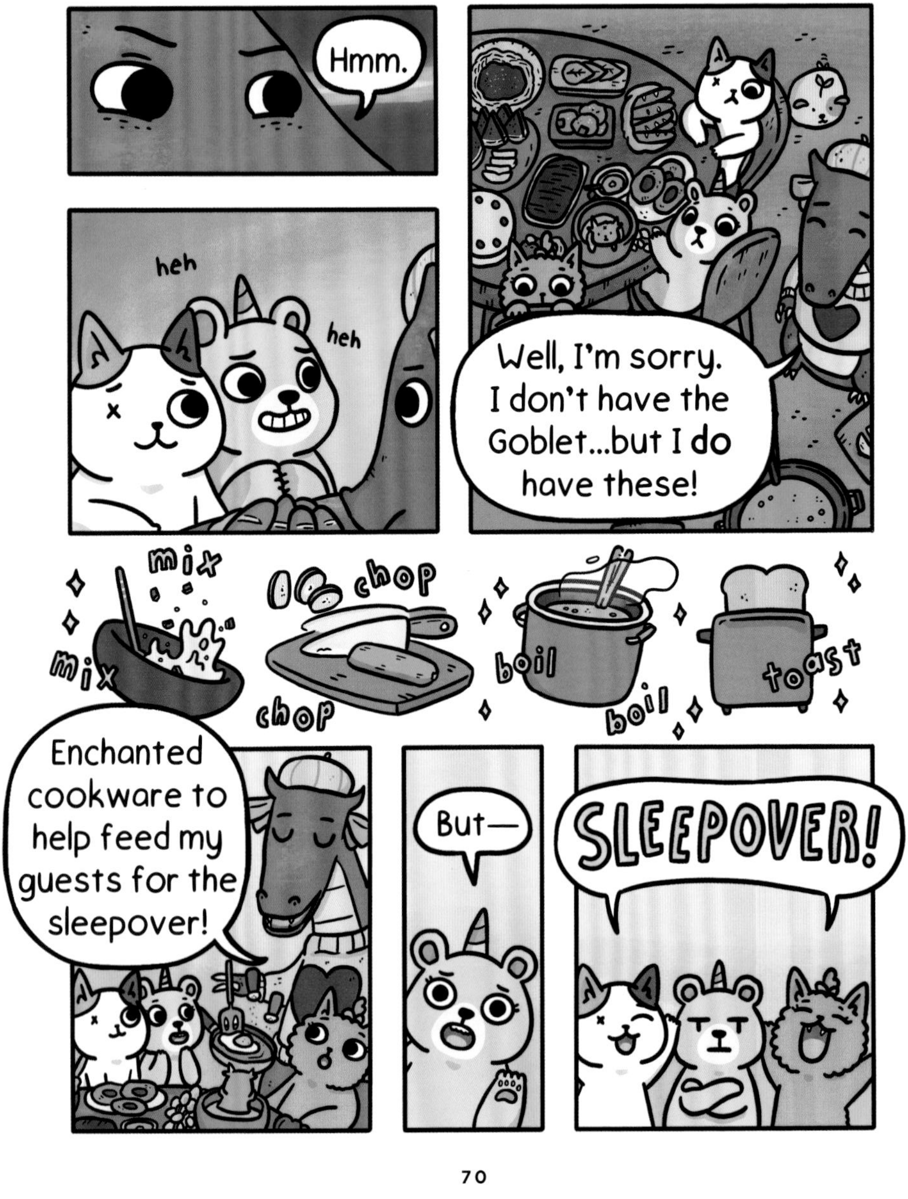

Hmm.
heh
heh
Well, I'm sorry. I don't have the Goblet...but I do have these!
mix
mix
chop
chop
boil
boil
toast
Enchanted cookware to help feed my guests for the sleepover!
But—
SLEEPOVER!

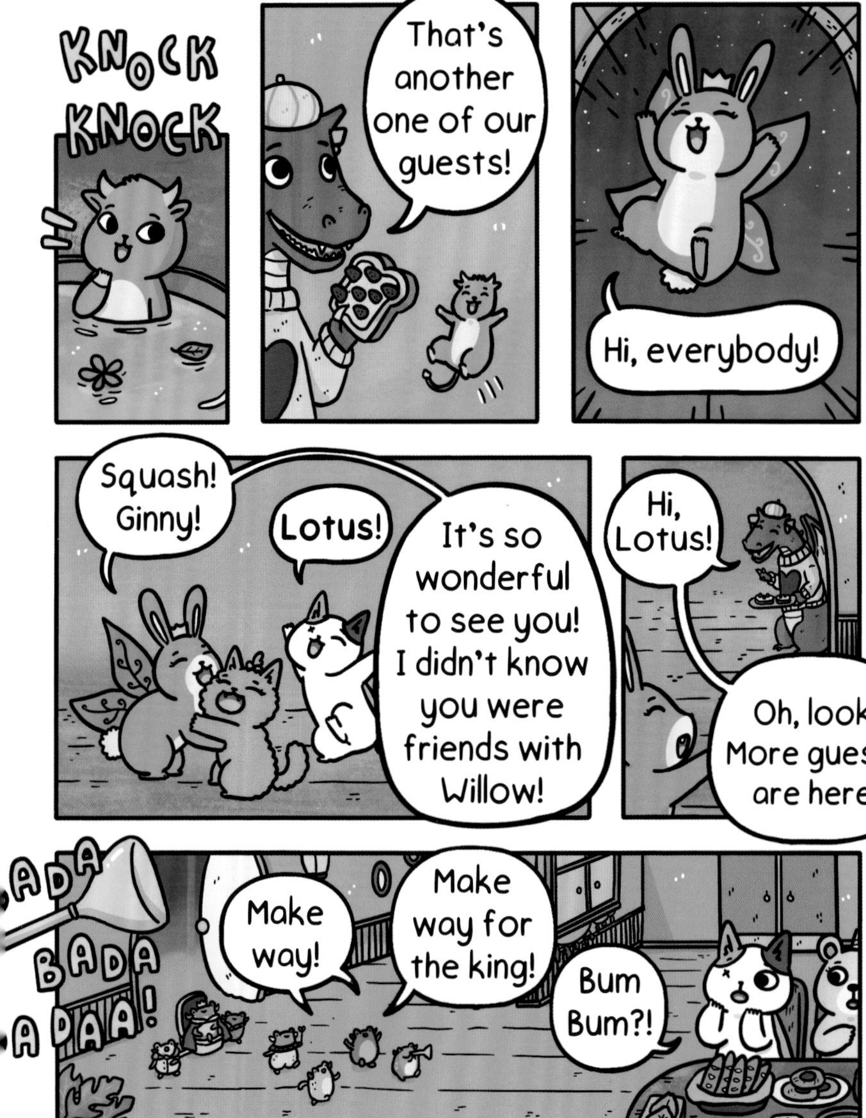
KNOCK KNOCK
That's another one of our guests!
Hi, everybody!
Squash! Ginny!
Lotus!
It's so wonderful to see you! I didn't know you were friends with Willow!
Hi, Lotus!
Oh, look! More guests are here!
BADA BADA BADAA!
Make way!
Make way for the king!
Bum Bum?!

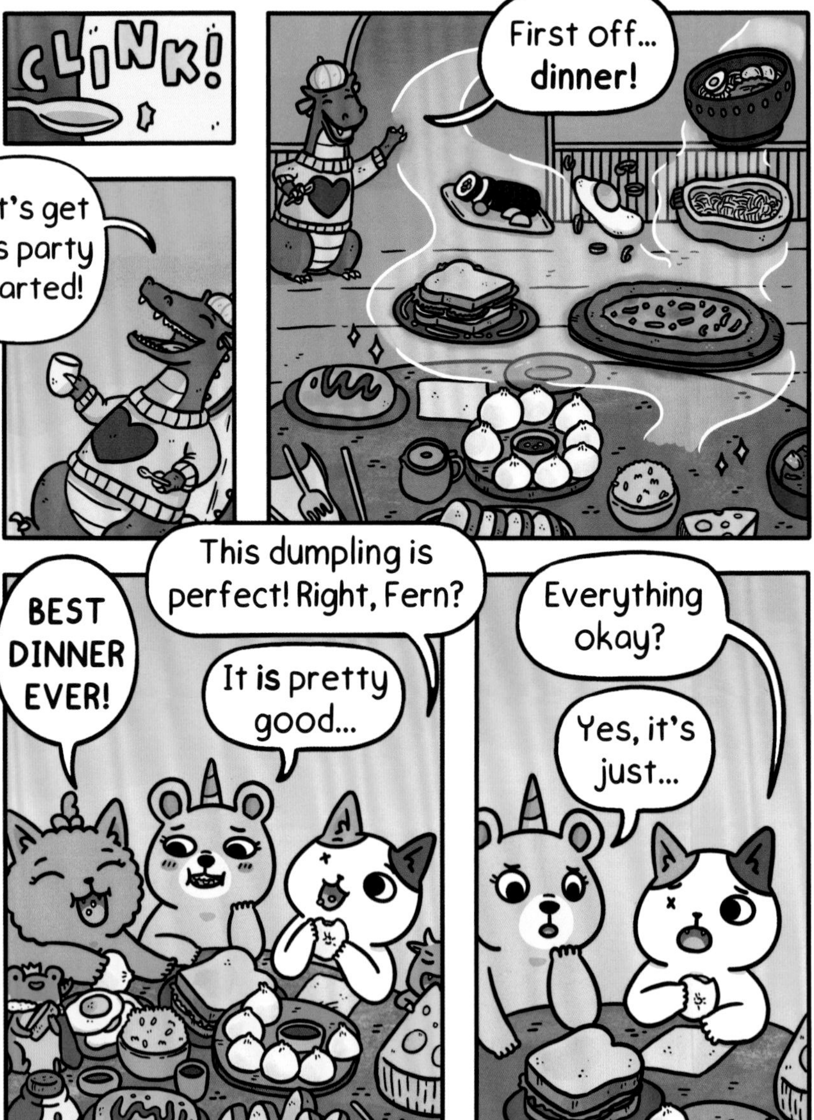
CLINK!
Let's get this party started!
First off... dinner!
BEST DINNER EVER!
This dumpling is perfect! Right, Fern?
It is pretty good...
Everything okay?
Yes, it's just...

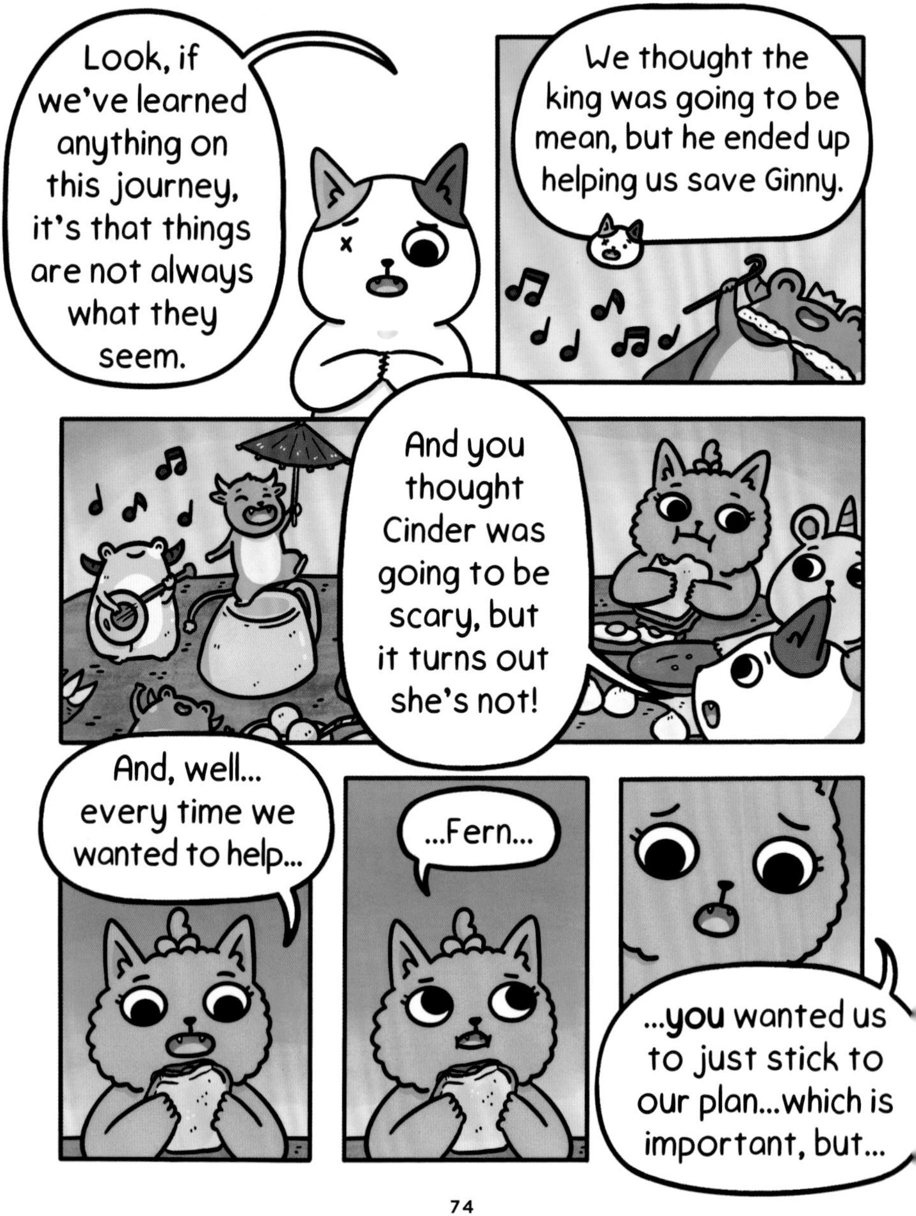
Look, if we've learned anything on this journey, it's that things are not always what they seem.
We thought the king was going to be mean, but he ended up helping us save Ginny.
And you thought Cinder was going to be scary, but it turns out she's not!
And, well... every time we wanted to help...
...Fern...
...**you** wanted us to just stick to our plan...which is important, but...

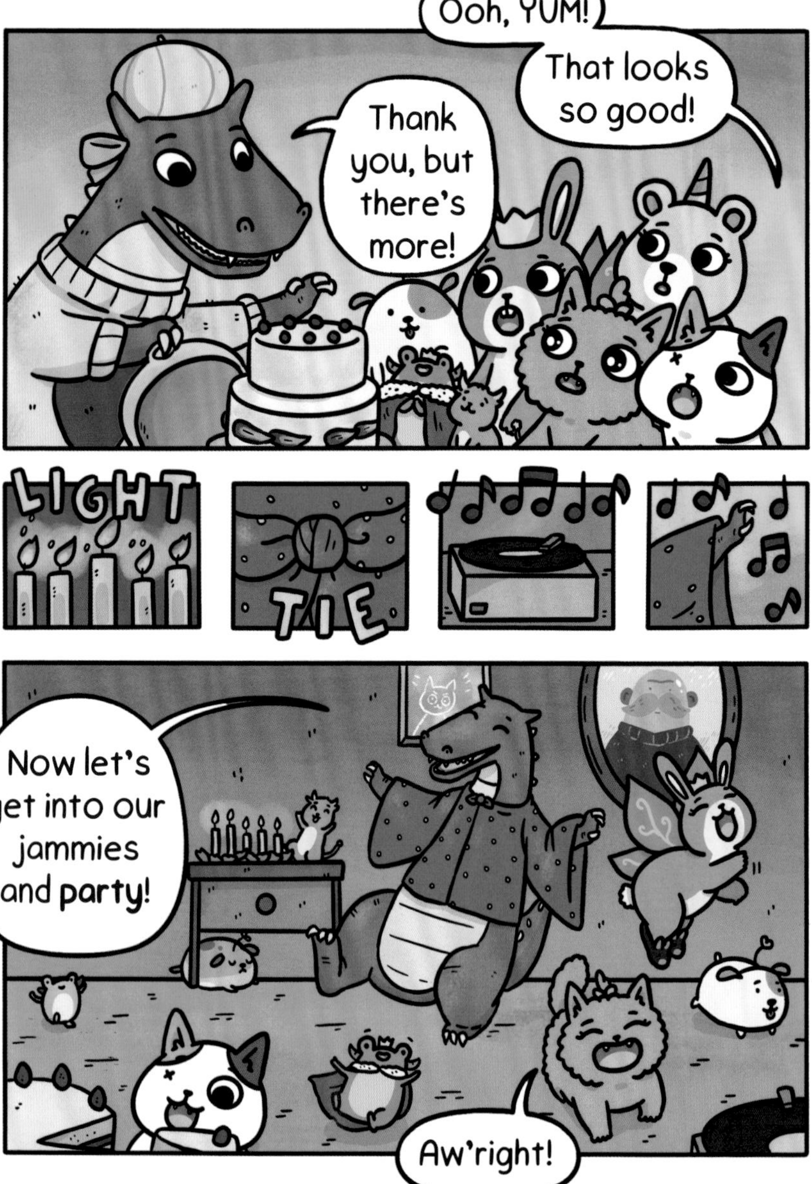
Ooh, YUM!
That looks so good!
Thank you, but there's more!
LIGHT
TIE
Now let's get into our jammies and **party**!
Aw'right!

CHAPTER SIX: The Truth

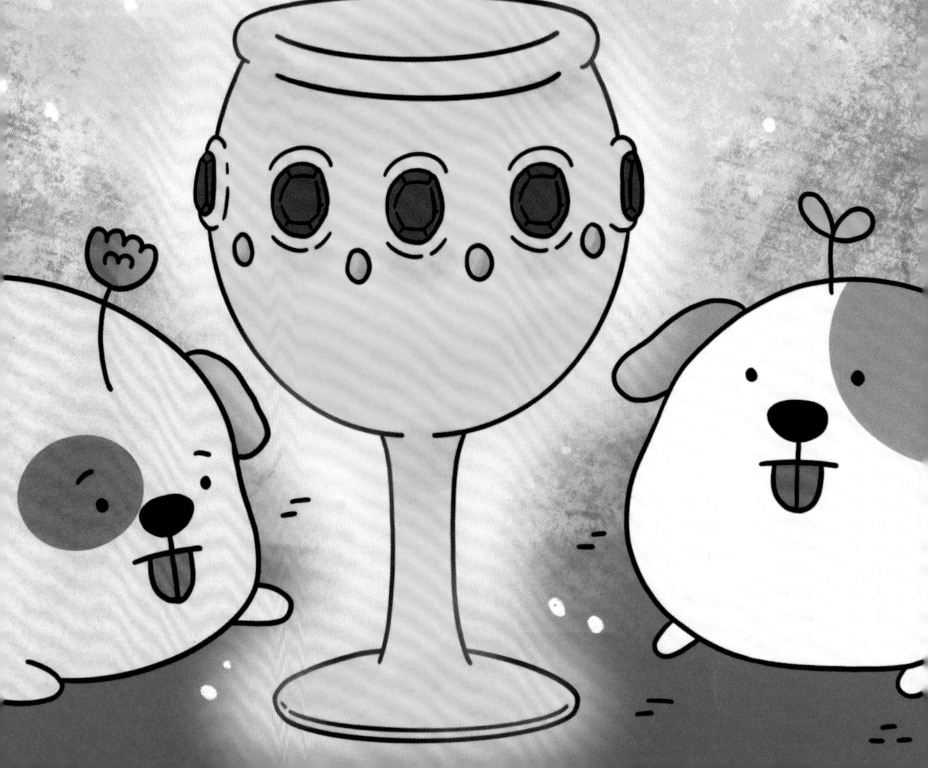

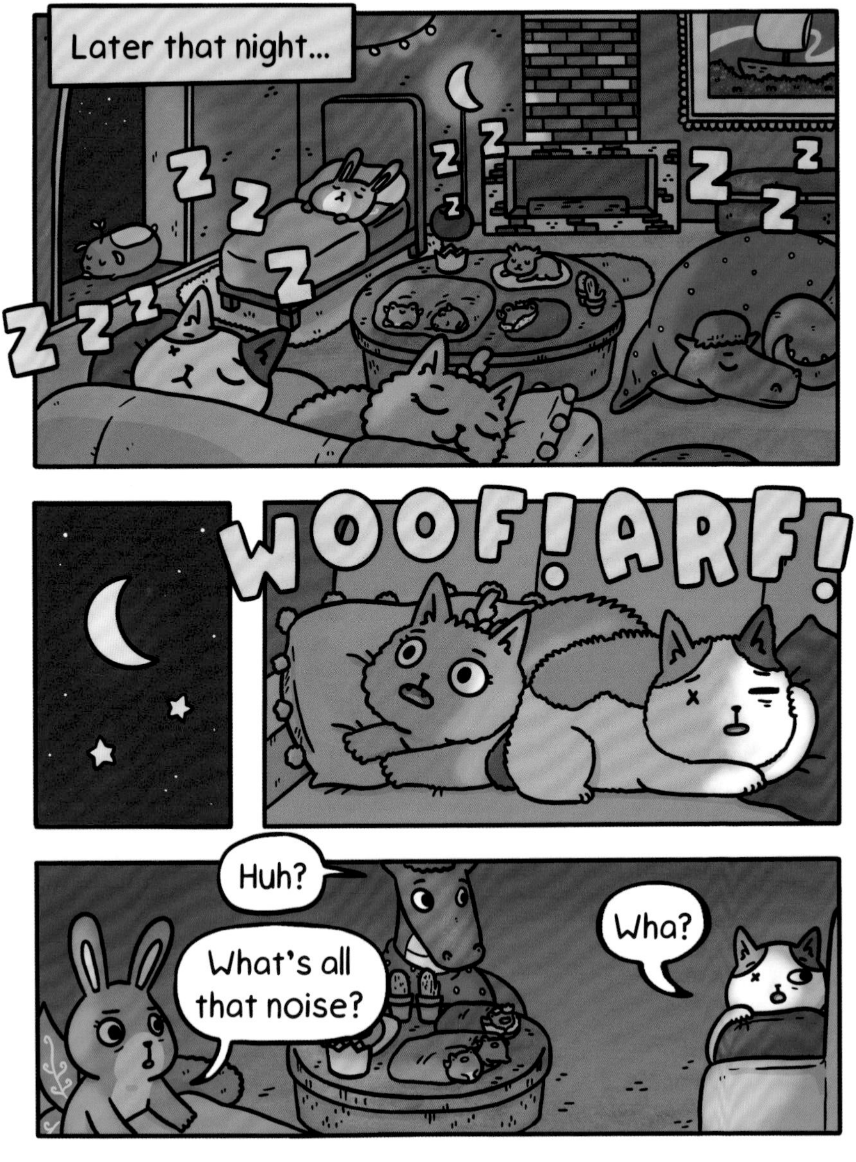
Later that night...
Z Z Z
WOOF! ARF!
Huh?
What's all that noise?
Wha?

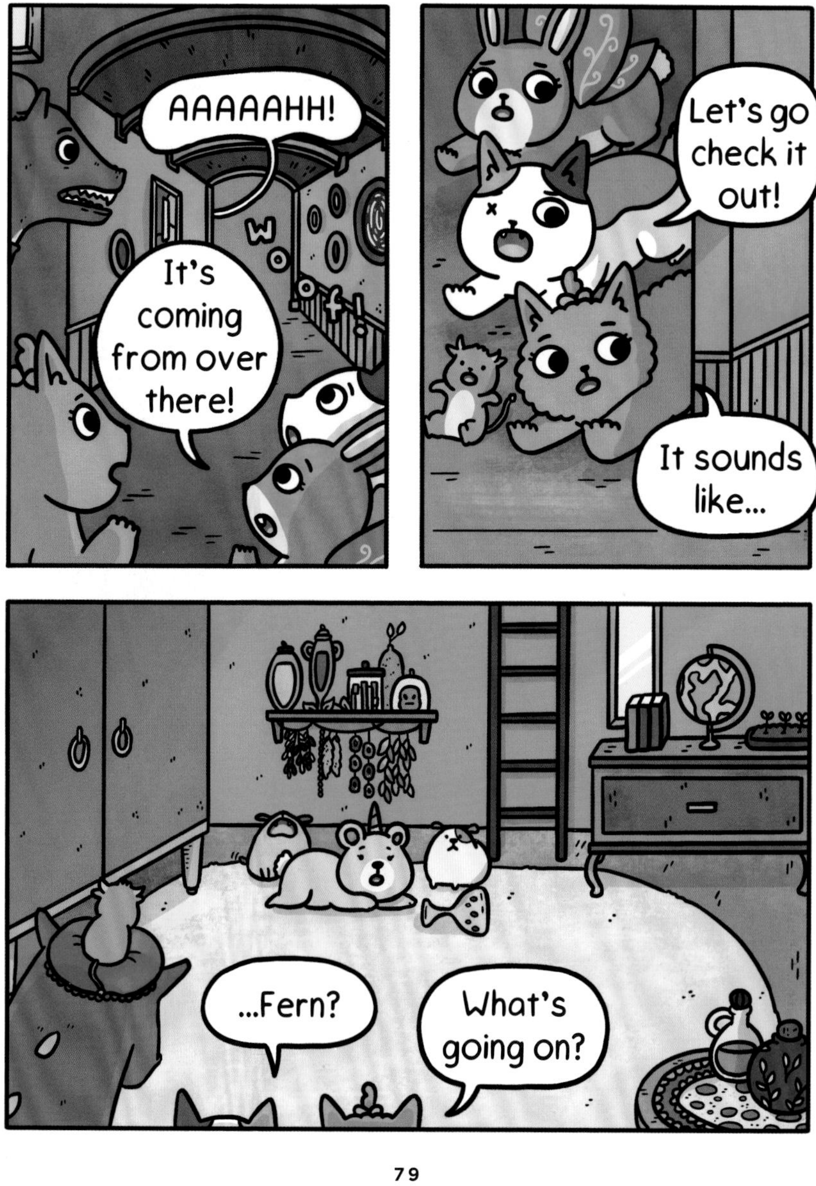
AAAAAHH!
Woof!
It's coming from over there!
Let's go check it out!
It sounds like...
...Fern?
What's going on?

83

84

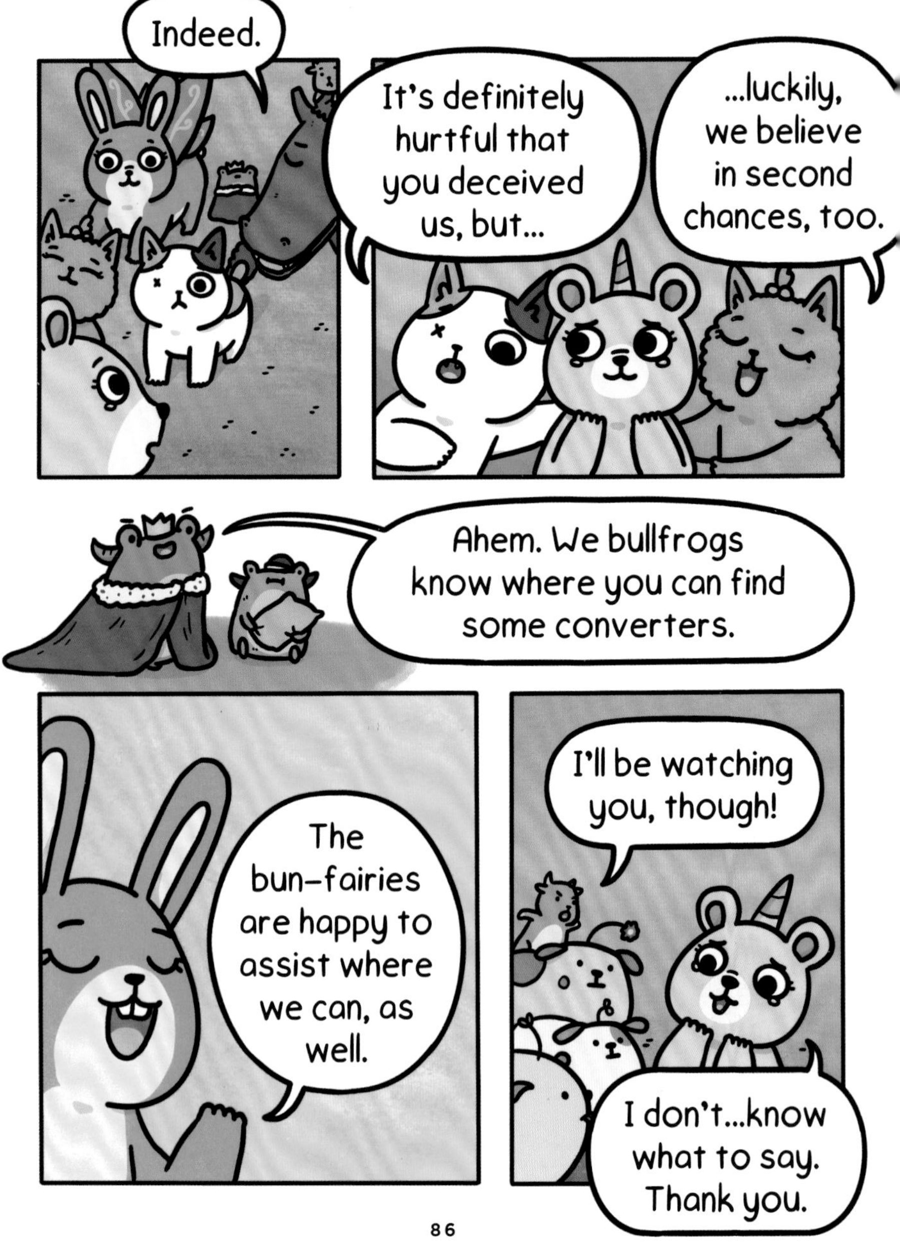
Indeed.
It's definitely hurtful that you deceived us, but...
...luckily, we believe in second chances, too.
Ahem. We bullfrogs know where you can find some converters.
The bun-fairies are happy to assist where we can, as well.
I'll be watching you, though!
I don't...know what to say. Thank you.

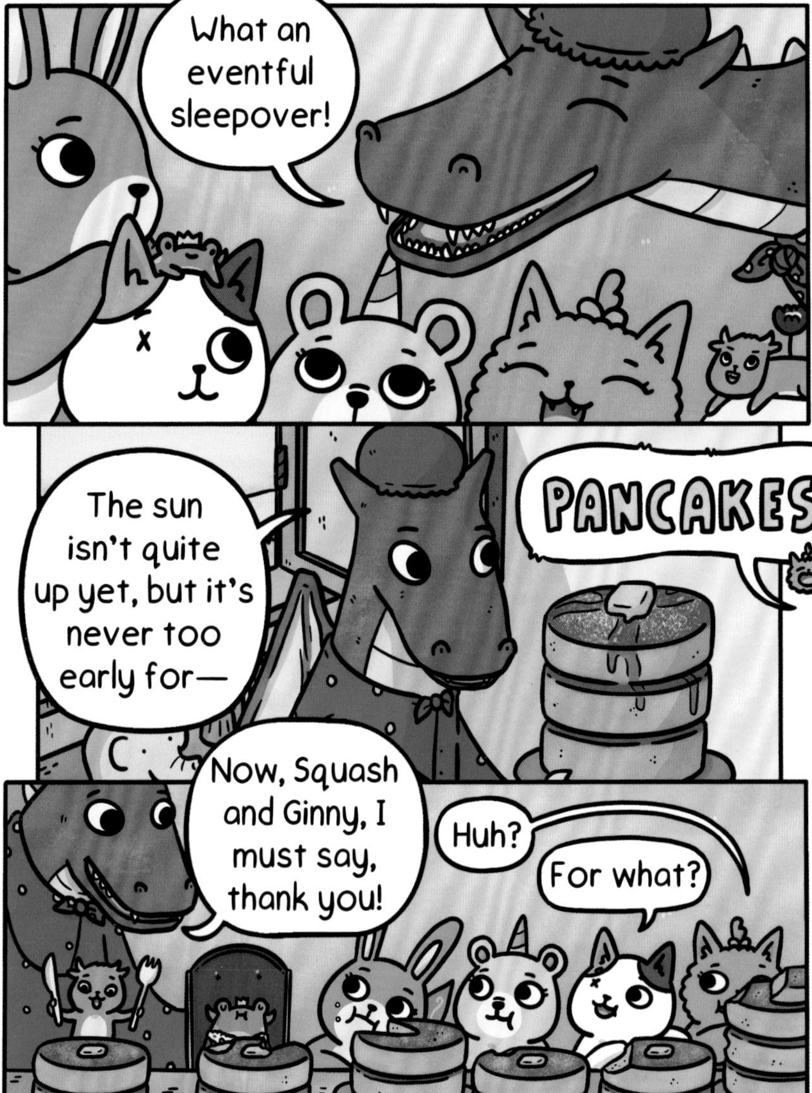
What an eventful sleepover!
The sun isn't quite up yet, but it's never too early for—
PANCAKES!
Now, Squash and Ginny, I must say, thank you!
Huh?
For what?

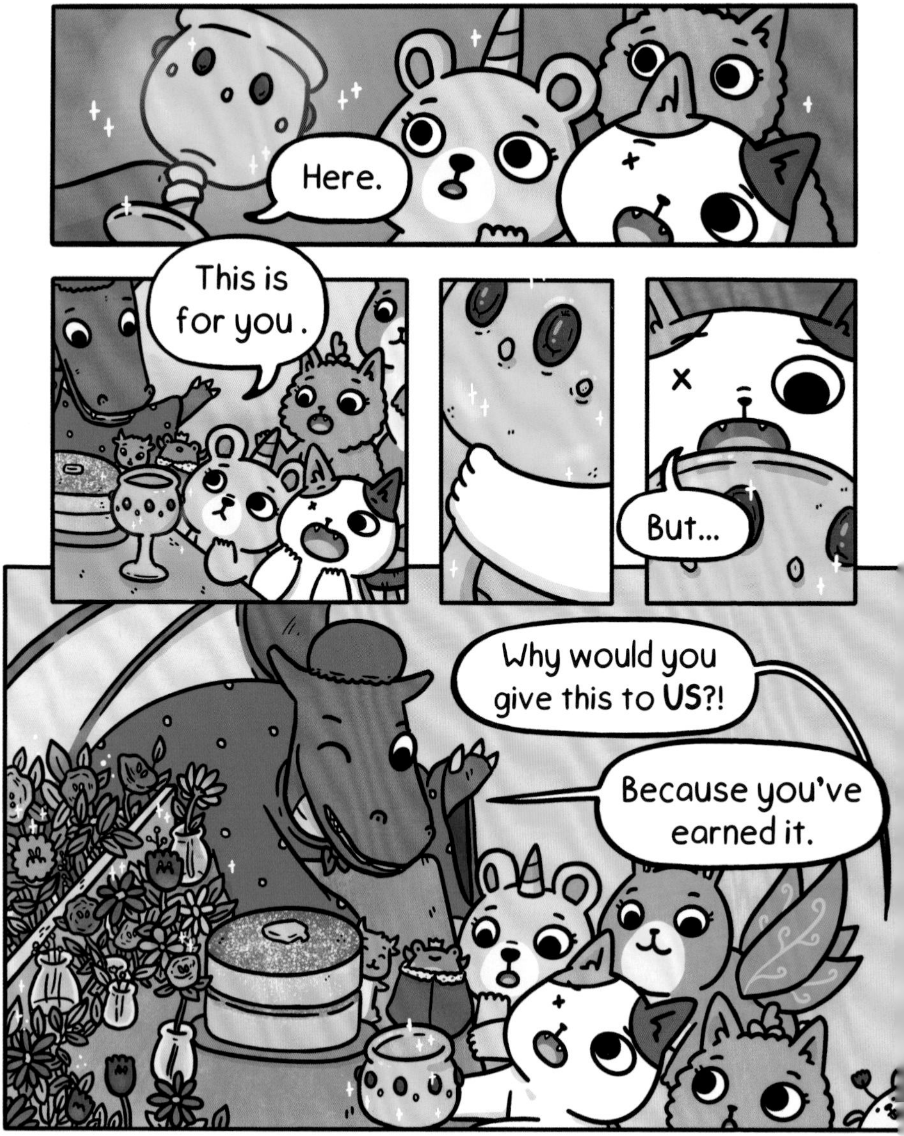
Here.
This is for you.
But...
Why would you give this to US?!
Because you've earned it.

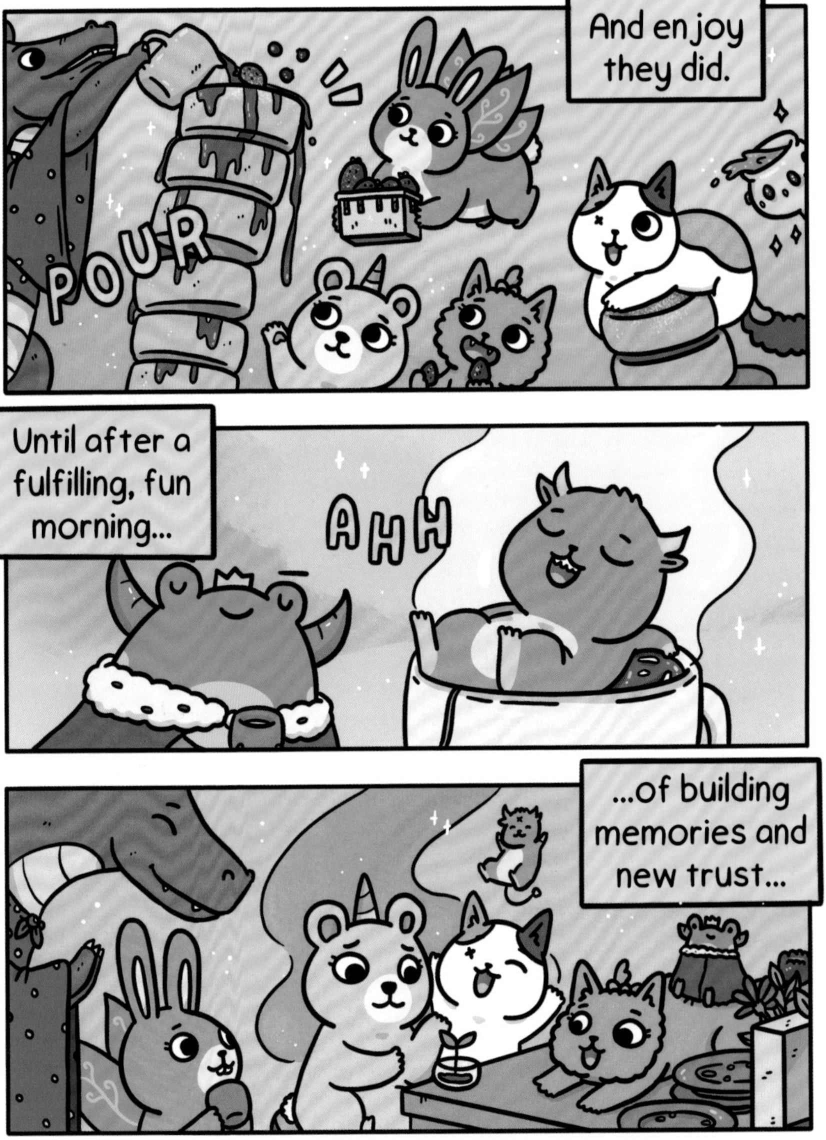
And enjoy they did.
POUR
Until after a fulfilling, fun morning...
AHH
...of building memories and new trust...

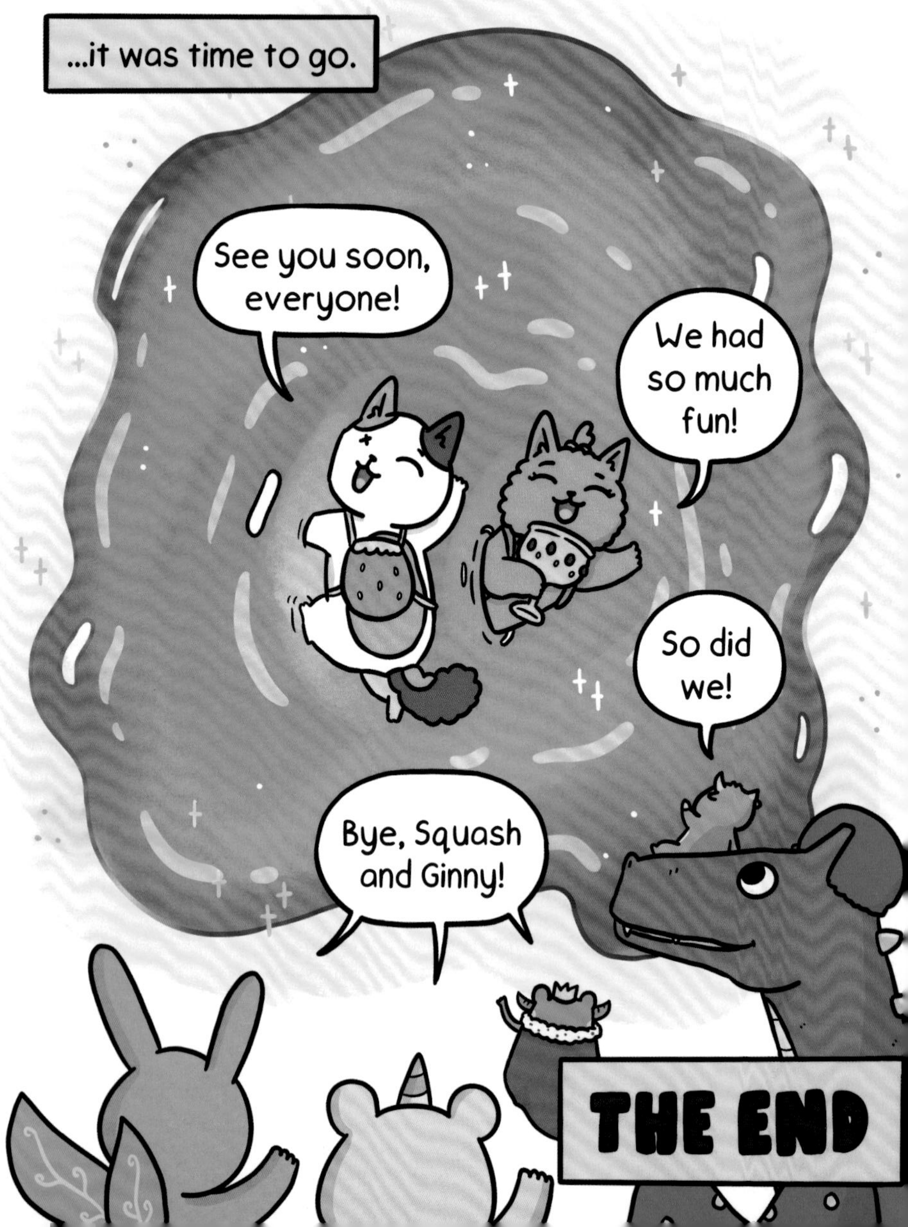
...it was time to go.
See you soon, everyone!
We had so much fun!
So did we!
Bye, Squash and Ginny!
THE END

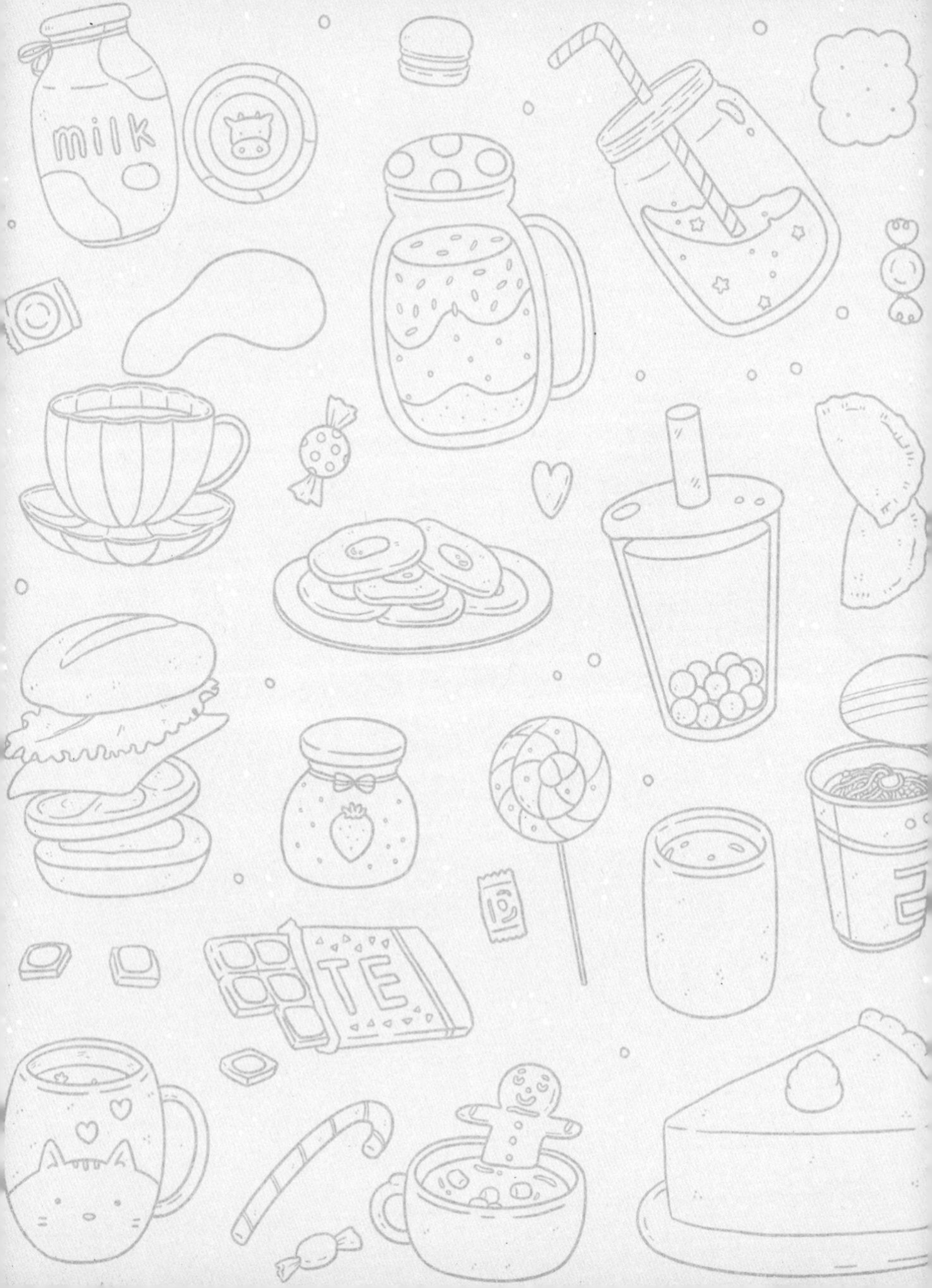
milk
TE